A Travel Guide for Reckless Hearts

ALSO BY N. M. KELBY

In the Company of Angels

Whale Season

Murder at the Bad Girl's Bar and Grill

Theater of the Stars:
A Novel of Physics and Memory

The Constant Art of Being a Writer:
The Life, Art and Business of Fiction

PRAISE FOR N. M. KELBY

"Kelby is a natural-born storyteller who manages to be
very funny and very wise at the same time."
CARL HIAASEN,
best-selling author and columnist
for the *Miami Herald*

"N. M. Kelby writes beautifully. Her characters are
unforgettable, and her use of oddball details adds to the
particular flavor of the story, which has moments of
melancholy and tenderness among the fireworks."
Capital Times

"Black humor that sizzles."
Kirkus Reviews

"Kelby puts forth divine miracles . . ."
Baltimore Sun

"To read Kelby's novel is, in its own words,
to fall into a dream."
New York Times Book Review

N. M. KELBY

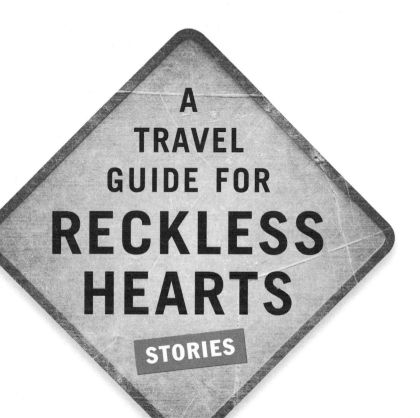

A
TRAVEL
GUIDE FOR
RECKLESS
HEARTS

STORIES

BOREALIS
BOOKS

Borealis Books is an imprint of the Minnesota Historical Society Press.

www.borealisbooks.org

The following stories have appeared elsewhere:
"Jubilation, Florida":
  NPR's *Selected Shorts: Travel Tales* and *New Stories from the South: The Year's Best, 2006*
"The Faithful":
  Minnesota Monthly
"We Are All Just Visitors Here":
  Chattahoochee Review
"Subtitled":
  Verb
"Deals":
  Mississippi Review
"Our Florida Vacation":
  Zoetrope: All-Story Extra
"Waiting for the Hungarians":
  West Branch

The Minnesota Historical Society Press is a member of the Association of American University Presses.

Manufactured in the United States of America.

10 9 8 7 6 5 4 3 2 1

∞ The paper used in this publication meets the minimum requirements of the American National Standard for Information Sciences—Permanence for Printed Library Materials, ANSI Z39.48-1984.

International Standard Book Number

ISBN-13: 978-0-87351-767-6 (paper)
ISBN-10: 0-87351-767-9 (paper)

Library of Congress Cataloging-in-Publication Data

Kelby, N. M. (Nicole M.)
A travel guide for reckless hearts / N. M. Kelby.
  p. cm.
ISBN-13: 978-0-87351-767-6
  (pbk : alk. paper)
ISBN-10: 0-87351-767-9
  (pbk : alk. paper)
I. Title.
PS3561.E382T73 2009
813'.54—dc22
                    2009019159

Cover design and photo collage:
  Percolator
Cover photo collage images:
Vintage sun rays—iStockphoto.com /
  Matt Knannlein
Old map—iStockphoto.com /
  Nikolay Staykov
Sign—iStockphoto.com /
  Julien Grondin
Palm tree—iStockphoto.com /
  Yong Hian Lim

A Travel Guide for Reckless Hearts

To Steven:
Every story begins and ends with your love.

A Travel Guide for Reckless Hearts

Jubilation, Florida

IT'S NOT A GOOD IDEA. Nordan and Sara both know it. Both are over forty. Both love their spouses. Both are drunk. Both naked—and not thin. Both wonder if the other is lying when they say, nearly simultaneously, "I've never done this before."

And they're friends—or think they are. It's difficult to tell. They were total strangers before they checked into adjoining hotel rooms in Jubilation, a planned community featuring Key West–styled homes in sherbet colors with white picket fences. The resort is Gingerbread Victorian, with a permit-only beach where the sand is raked into traditional Zen patterns three times a day. There are no homeless people in Jubilation. No tattoo shops. There's nothing sordid, or dangerous. You can't even walk down the side streets unless you have security clearance; surveillance cameras are everywhere. It's not the kind of place you'd have an affair in.

But here they are, naked—and a little cold. It's off-season.

"Two things before we go any further," Nordan says—all business, all courage, all confidence. In the moonlight, his goose bumps are disconcerting, make him look a little like a plucked turkey.

"I want to be clear. My wife is so great; I don't even have

a pool because I'm afraid she'd run off with the pool guy.
Mary Anne is the most glorious control freak on Earth.
Kicked my ass into shape. I have to warn you, if she finds out
about this, she'll hunt you down like a feral dog and chew
your heart out."

Sara is unfazed. Doesn't even blink. "That's a given," she
says. "More bourbon?" She pours the last of it before he can
answer. Nordan takes a mouthful, swallows it so fast he
coughs.

An alarmed look passes over Sara's face. "We don't have
to do this."

"No. I want you. I want to."

"So, what's the second thing?"

"The second thing is that I would never leave my wife.
For all her goofy shit, she's fierce. Not many women like that
anymore."

Sara is relieved. She takes a sip from Nordan's glass, looks
at him closely—the plucked skin, the pleading eyes, the
"What the hell am I doing?" look on his face. She has no idea
how she's going to explain this to her therapist.

"Okay," she says. "There are two things you should know."

"Fair enough."

"First, my husband is the kindest, most gentle man I have
ever met. I clearly don't deserve him. He's like a surfing,
golfing St. Francis of Assisi. If he ever finds out, he may want
to kill you, but he's so kindhearted, and not very well organ-
ized, so he couldn't pull it off. I'd have to do it. I'm kind of his
'go-to' gal. Just thought you should know."

"Noted. The second thing?"

"Well, afterwards, I'm planning to burn your body and sprinkle your ashes on my roses."

"Makes sense."

"Absolutely. Bone marrow is a superior fertilizer, plus I've kind of gotten used to you hanging around—so, it would be the best of both worlds," she says, then corrects. "Well, for me, of course. You'd be mulch."

It is at this moment that Nordan realizes why people should not talk before having sex.

"Okay," he says. "That's—"

He is fumbling for just the right word, one that won't ruin whatever shreds of desire remain. He decides on "sweet," and she smiles, which encourages him so he just keeps on talking. "Yep. That's sort of sweet. Twisted, but slightly endearing."

Sara looks so beautiful standing there in front of him, like a freaking Botticelli, so it makes him nervous. Her skin reminds him of vanilla ice cream, not the no-fat crap, the expensive stuff with 27 percent saturated fat—the Lipitor-inducing stuff. He'd like to tell her that, but already has, and doesn't want to repeat himself. Might ruin the moment. So he tries to remember a poem by James Dickey about adultery. Something about not being able to die in this room, about having this moment only, stealing a little bit more life from life. Nordan would like to remember this poem because he knows it would be the perfect thing to say, but he's had so much bourbon all he can manage is, "Said the raven. Nevermore."

Sara looks confused. Nordan's mood turns frantic; he

hopes she isn't having second thoughts. "Nevermore," he says again, as if trying to make a point. Better to bluff, he thinks, than look like an idiot.

"Great," Sara says. *What am I doing with this idiot?*

Nordan can feel her doubt. He shrugs, looks a little sheepish, and slaps himself on the forehead—and that changes everything. Suddenly, it's clear to Sara that this man has crawled into her brain, pitched a tent, and, somehow, is a part of her now. It's too late to turn back, so she takes the glass out of his hand and pulls him into her arms.

"Maybe we can stop talking now," she whispers, throaty, and before he can say anything else, she kisses him. Open mouth. Greedy.

He shudders with pleasure, fear. They both do, actually.

Neither is quite sure how they got to this point.

Sara and Nordan are supposed to be on a retreat. They've both won this year's Bennington Foundation Leadership Award, along with twenty-two others. It's a very prestigious award. There's no application process, nomination only. Leaders from both the arts and sciences are chosen every year.

Nordan was honored for his work as a consultant who teaches poetry to business executives from Fortune 500 companies. He once told Ed Bradley on *60 Minutes* that poetry in the workplace humanizes and makes change. "It's the ultimate form of revolution," he said, and then called it a "slick gig," and drove off in his Maserati.

The piece was titled, "Corporate America's Abbie Hoffman."

Sara's award was given because she'd written a memoir about her own personal search for grace. It was elegant and heartfelt and more or less true.

Sara is one of those women. Big boned. Bleached blonde. Seems taller than she is. She'd been a police beat reporter for the CNN affiliate in the Twin Cities for nearly twenty years.

She'd been shot at while covering drug raids. Beaten up at a race riot. She once went undercover at a strip joint and knows that pasties hurt if you pull them off too quickly.

When Sara turned forty, she wasn't interested in a monthly regime of Botox, as the news director suggested, so she left television to write a memoir. Her agent cautioned her that she'd need a new angle, something fresh.

"Maybe you could join a convent or something."

So she did. Sara was between husbands at the time, her second had just left, so living with cloistered nuns seemed to make a lot of sense. "I'll spend a lot less on makeup," she told her friends. The book proposal created a bidding war between publishers and brought a high-six-figure contract. But once the check was cashed, reality set in. All that kneeling, and not speaking, and averting one's eyes drove Sara crazy after three weeks, so she left—but wrote the book anyway.

"They've taken a vow of silence," she told her agent. "It's not like they'll tell anyone."

Cloistered was a *New York Times* best seller for a week. That was in 2000, the same year she married Mike—who is ten years younger, takes in stray animals, volunteers at soup kitchens, and has no marketable job skills. Sara hasn't written a thing since. She and Mike are just about out of money, but that's okay. The leadership award provides a guaranteed income of $100,000 a year, for two years.

Which is good for Nordan, too. He recently came to the rude discovery that he's fallen out of fashion, is now forced to teach at a community college.

So Nordan and Sara have come to Jubilation to get the check, although the foundation director would not describe the situation so indelicately. According to the website, every year, before the money is given out, award recipients are brought together at resorts around the country, and for fourteen days they take part in networking sessions with titles like, "How to Unleash Your Inner Leader."

"It is our desire to create a think-tank atmosphere," the foundation director is quoted as saying. "When you make it easy for leaders to cross-pollinate, their communities will benefit tenfold."

Sara and Nordan are pretty sure this is not the kind of cross-pollination the director had in mind.

"Well," Nordan says.

"Well," Sara echoes.

Outside, a seagull squawks.

When they were first introduced, Nordan told Sara he was the biggest egomaniac she would ever meet. He meant it as a joke, but he is. And she knows it. And yet, here they are—Sara standing at the edge of the bed watching Nordan watch her. Her lips are now bruised from his. Her breasts, full and round.

"Just like those little cheese wheels," Nordan says. "The ones in red wax. Gouda, is it?"

Sara guesses that's a compliment, but it's difficult to tell. She's lactose intolerant. "Sure," she says. She'd like to say something more, something to compliment him, but she knows of no cheese product that Nordan reminds her of, and he's told her repeatedly that he hates compliments.

"I'm a realist," he said. "There were two years in college when I was handsome. The baby fat had dropped away, and I played NCAA basketball with a full head of hair that wasn't implanted from somewhere else. Now, I'm one hot fudge sundae away from morphing into Jabba the Hutt."

Nordan is clearly a man who likes his dairy.

Sara finds it hard to believe Nordan is completely unaware that he is still handsome, still has an athlete's grace. His body may have grown thick with age, but it's powerful and muscular. His broad chest is covered with golden hair, like fleece. He reminds her of a lion. Sara's never seen anything quite like Nordan. Her husband Mike is smooth and nearly hairless, like a boy. Nordan is sweaty, unwieldy, and passionate. He shudders when she touches him, which is a little unnerving. It makes her wonder if he's been in prison for the last seven years instead of a suburb in Connecticut.

Of course, she thinks, soccer moms and prison guards both carry whistles. Lights out by 9 PM. This is why she doesn't live in the suburbs.

Still, when Nordan lifts her into his arms and kisses her, she is lost in it. It feels as if they are skydiving through each other's lives.

"This is such a bad idea," he says.

"You're right," she says.

But they don't stop.

For the past two weeks, Nordan and Sara have spent every night drinking and watching the sun set in what could only be described as a boozy filibuster haze. They never seemed to stop talking. They talked about the NBA, the NFL, rock and roll, Japanese baseball teams, his career, his dreams, his ambitions, his wife Mary Anne's obsessive love of Lilly Pulitzer resortwear ("She's wearing pink flamingos in Connecticut, for chrissake"), and his uncle, a five-hundred-pound circus clown with narcolepsy. Funny stories, nothing too sad. Their talks seemed like an endless cocktail party, but every now and then one or the other would say, "Shit, I can't believe I'm telling you this. I've never told anybody this."

And then they'd both stop talking.

On day six, Sara confessed that when she was seven years old, she actually believed she could grow up to be a super-hero. She was laughing when she told Nordan she'd climbed onto the roof of her family's double-wide trailer with a bed sheet wrapped around her neck and jumped, breaking her right leg.

She expected Nordan to laugh too, but he was quiet.

"It's a true story. I swear," she said. "What kind of an ego-maniac believes they're a superhero?"

Nordan cleared his throat. "In my case," he said, "it was a garage. I was eight. It was my sister's blanket and my left foot."

Sara looked concerned. "Shit," she said. "Do you ever wonder why we're on this porch? You and I? It's not some sort of destiny thing, is it? I'd hate that. I don't even read my horoscope."

Nordan thought about it a minute, then shook his head. "Naw. We're here because we're poseurs. We have to stick together." Then he poured her another bourbon.

That's when Sara decided she liked Nordan.

Yet, in all those drunken nights, she never imagined having sex with him, even though they had adjoining rooms. Then, on night thirteen, things changed.

It began rather innocently. Sara fell asleep in her wicker chair while Nordan was rambling on about steroids and batting averages. So he picked her up in his massive arms and carried her into her room—and she's not exactly a small woman. "Time for bed, Slugger," he said and placed her gently on top of the sheets. He brushed her hair out of her eyes and covered her with a blanket. Then kissed her forehead. "Sweet dreams," he said.

The noble gentleness of the gesture, the quiet innocence of it, stunned her. Who is this guy, really? She suddenly wanted to find out. So the next night, their last night together, Sara called for a "no-bullshit zone."

"Tell me about Seth," she said. Seth is Nordan's only child, from his first marriage. He just turned fourteen. "You said his birthday was last Saturday, right? What's he like?"

Nordan looked surprised. "I can't believe I mentioned Seth, let alone his birthday. But, hell, you know me: I don't listen to a word I say—"

"Shut up then and tell me about him."

"What's to tell? Seth's my kid. A real slacker, like his old man. When he comes to visit, we hide out together in the basement and watch ESPN. I bitch about the Lakers. He pisses about the Timberwolves. It's pretty great."

"Do you see him a lot?"

"Every other Christmas. Every other summer."

"Is that hard?"

"It just is. How about you? You have kids?"

"Just one," she said. "Hannah. She died a long time ago."

Nordan wasn't expecting that at all. "Jesus. How old?"

"Six days."

"How long ago?"

"Fourteen years."

"That's horrible."

"It just is. Hannah suffocated in her crib. The mattress was too soft. I didn't know."

Nordan reached over to take Sara's hand, but she moved it away.

"I'm fine. It was a long time ago."

What Sara didn't say was that she could have saved Hannah. She heard her baby fussing, but didn't get up to check on her. She was too tired. So Hannah died. Right in the next room. Hannah with her perfect fingers and buttermilk skin. Her Buddha eyes. And it was Sara's fault. But she didn't have to tell Nordan any of this, because he heard it in her voice— all the details she couldn't speak—and that scared him. So they sat in silence and watched the moon slip in and out of the clouds. They rocked back and forth. The chairs creaked. After a time Nordan said, "Your daughter and my son would have been about the same age."

"Sorry I brought it up."

"No, it's good. I just realized that they could have dated. Man, would that be something, or what? Your kid would speak five languages and mine would show her how to dye her hair rainbow colors with Jell-O. Wouldn't that be something?"

Sara didn't know what to say. She never thought of Hannah as a young girl, or dating. But as soon as Nordan said it, she did. She imagined evenings spent with Nordan, driving around in her Jeep, looking for their kids in tattoo shops, or behind the bleachers at football games.

"It would be something," she said and laughed and leaned over and kissed Nordan on the cheek.

"Thanks," he said gratefully, just as he had earlier at dinner when she had handed him her piece of Key lime pie, which she remembered, at the last minute, contains sweetened condensed milk.

"You're all right," he said then.

"I'm lactose intolerant."

"Well, you're all right, too."

And then she laughed.

And hours later, when she kissed him out of gratitude for this vision of Hannah, he said it again. "You're all right." Then kissed her back, quickly. "Bruised as hell, just like me, but all right."

And then she unbuttoned her shirt.

That's how it all began. Nordan carried her into his room and placed her on his bed. They undressed in silence. They tried to make small talk, but much of it revolved around dairy products. And now, three hours later, somewhere around 2:00 AM, after speaking about Gouda cheese at great length, Nordan finally finds his courage, runs his teeth along her neck, her breasts.

Sara feels her skin swell under them, feels him grow hard against her leg.

Nordan's thoughts bounce like tennis balls. It'll be great. Nobody will get hurt. It's only sex. No big deal. Game. Set. Match.

Love.

He stops, again. Shudders. Then holds her so tightly she can barely breathe. For some reason, he suddenly can't seem to let go.

"What's wrong?"

"Shh."

"You okay?"

"Give me a minute, I'll be fine."

His breath is rapid, and for the first time in a long time Nordan feels afraid. He has no idea why. When the moment finally passes, he lets her fall out of his arms. "That was weird," he says, his voice hoarse. "I just had this feeling like there's a storm raging around us, and I didn't even know it was raining."

The moment feels airless.

"I better go," Sara says and stands. "I have an early plane to catch."

"Right."

Nordan picks up her bra from the floor and looks at it for a moment. "We still friends?"

"Sure."

The word feels brittle. Nordan catches her arm. "Look,

I don't know what the hell's going on, but when you touch me, I don't hate it. I always hate to be touched—"

"I have to go."

"I'm talking too much again, aren't I?"

"It's an early flight."

"Okay. Here's the deal," he says, and then stops. Takes a deep breath. "I get you. And underneath all my bullshit, you get me, too."

And it's true. Sara knows it. So she runs. She runs out onto the porch and out the screen door and onto the perfectly groomed Zen-themed beach.

And Nordan follows her.

And they're both naked.

And it's April.

And the air temperature is sixty-nine degrees, with a light chop off the Gulf.

Nordan and Sara are still a little drunk, and working off adrenaline, so they aren't thinking about any of this. Nor are they thinking about the "Caution, No Swimming" sign they pass, nor that it's nesting season for sea turtles.

And, most of all, they aren't thinking about the fact that the Red Cross suggests the optimal temperature for Gulf water is about eighty degrees. Colder than that, and you risk hypothermia. It's a very slim risk in Florida, but still. Maybe Nordan and Sara don't know that. Either way, it doesn't matter. It's seventy-two degrees when Sara dives in, and Nordan blindly follows. Once wet, it's quite clear that the Red Cross knows exactly what it's talking about.

"Yeow!" they both scream.

Nordan lunges for Sara out of a primal need—for warmth, mostly—and pulls her close to his hairy body. He's panting hard from the cold and feels his heart beat in his teeth when he asks, "Would it be better if I told you I just wanted to 'do' you? I could say that."

Sara laughs and a cloud moves away from the moon. The night shimmers. "Look, sea turtles," she says and points to the beach.

There are five, perhaps six; it's difficult to tell. They are lumbering mountains, some as big as Nordan, maybe two hundred pounds or more. A few swim in the waters nearby, mating. They are graceful as they circle each other, but nearly drown as they try to mount.

"They're worse than us," Nordan says.

"Shh," Sara laughs.

The hotel lobby, and also the beach, has signs that warn guests not to swim at night and not to make any noise or use flashlights when walking the shore. Sea turtles are endangered.

"Any disruption of their mating could have serious long-term implications," the signs state in large red letters. Nordan suddenly remembers that, and wonders what the "implications" are, and who should be more worried about them—the turtles or the swimmers. He pulls Sara closer, and watches. The turtles are terrifying and beautiful, uncaring as gods.

"They live to be a hundred years old," Sara whispers, "and come to the same spot every year to mate."

Apparently, they've not heard of Club Med, Nordan

thinks, but remembers a verse from Song of Songs, at least thinks he does, and says, "I will arise now and go about the city in the streets and seek him whom my soul loveth."

Sara kisses his cheek. "I love you," she says simply.

The words sound so sweet, a horrible panicked look crosses Nordan's face.

"Calm down," Sara says. "I love you like pie. Like Key lime pie."

"But you're lactose intolerant."

"That's the breaks."

And so he kisses her hard. And she, him.

And for a long time they hold each other and watch the turtles and their awkward dance. They watch until their fingers go numb, then their feet, then hands, then legs.

They watch until they can't feel a thing.

◆

The Faithful

THE ICE IS SILVER: tarnished and spotty in the moonlight. Harvey, my mother's second husband, not my father, has just gassed up the chainsaw. It screeches to life, all teeth and danger.

My mother, whom we have all referred to as "Kitty" since the early 1970s, pops open a bottle of Moët & Chandon. "Merry Christmas," she laughs up and down the scale. Champagne overflows onto her lap, then rolls off the coyote fur she's wrapped around herself for warmth. The coat is old. It sheds in handfuls. She is sitting on the edge of the frozen lake on a chaise lounge. She is wearing a bathing suit, the color of a summer sky, but you can't see it. The coat covers all.

It's their last Christmas here. Harvey and my mother are retiring to a condo in Orlando, Florida. "We hear the call of the mouse," Harvey likes to say. Then, often, he sings the theme to *The Mickey Mouse Club.*

"Who's the leader of the club that's made for you and me?"

I try not to answer.

Harvey and my mother are selling everything: the business, the house, and this small lake, which has no name.

I still call it Dad's Lake, because my father had it dug. He loved it. The house winds around a good portion of it. I suspect, as "waterfront property," the house will bring good money. The ad in the newspaper referred to it as an "executive retreat."

I'm afraid to touch anything. Everything feels for sale.

On the shore, just a few feet away, the bonfire is edgy. Bits of old doors and lumber from the barn fuel the fire. It arcs, snaps at the sky.

Kitty, my mother—the phrase always fills me with amazement. Now, at this moment, even more so. She's wearing cat's-eye sunglasses, despite the fact that it's dark out, and a long white scarf wrapped around her head. It's her usual. She's worn that same Lana Turner look since she was seventeen years old. She looks like nobody's mother, but has two children. I have a younger sister, Josie, who no longer speaks to either of us.

I hold the paper cups out for Mother to pour. For a moment, the chainsaw sputters, coughs. And then goes quiet. My ears still ring from it. Overhead, the squawking of geese, late leaving, goes unheard.

"Need any help, Harvey?" I shout over my shoulder, though I don't know anything about chainsaws. He shakes his silver head. Pulls the cord again. The saw jerks back and hits the ice, chewing. Black diamonds fly into the Minnesota night.

"Harvey never needs help, darling. He's a determined man," my mother says. She should know. Harvey is also my uncle. He and Dad, born a year apart, looked nearly identical. Like twins, some said.

"So shoot me," she said when she married Harvey last year.

Nobody came to the wedding, not even me. It isn't that I don't like Harvey. He's great. Not my father, but great. *Really great*—that's what I told Kitty. "Just really great."

She hung up the phone.

Now, nearly a year later, under the shy new moon, Kitty looks all World War II pretty again, just as she was when she and my father met at the USO. He was a sailor on the USS *Intrepid*, an aircraft carrier. The *Intrepid* is huge, an Essex class carrier.

"It was my brush with greatness," he told me.

I grew up in the shadow of it.

When Josie and I were kids, Dad told us all about the Big Boat. It was the one bedtime story we never grew tired of. He told us about how hard it was to land the bombers on the flight deck at night in the middle of the sea, in the middle of nowhere.

"In that thick ink, the ocean and sky blurred into each other," he said. "Runway lights looked like stars. The stars just looked away. Worst of all, everything smelled of gas and smoke. Always. Creeps into your dreams."

The USS *Intrepid* was the backbone battleship of World War II, and then Vietnam. Between the wars, it was the primary recovery vessel for NASA. But, in the 1970s, it was retired. Relegated to rust. The summer after it happened, right before my senior year in high school, Dad drove us all to the boatyard to say our farewells. It was the only vacation he ever took with us, if you could call it that. He wore his old dog tags and made my sister and me say a prayer. I blew a kiss. Kitty held him tightly, and wept. It was the first time I could remember seeing her cry, or seeing them embrace.

Then, in 1982, the most amazing thing happened. The *Intrepid* became a floating museum in New York City's harbor. Renamed the Intrepid Sea, Air & Space Museum, it was docked in the Hudson River and open to the public.

As soon as I heard, I felt we should all go together to see it. I proposed a family vacation.

"Just like the last time," I said, enraptured by nostalgia. "Just the four of us."

Dad's face turned hard. "Me and the Big Boat have a lot in common," he said. "But nobody wants to see me float again."

"But it would be fun."

"No. It would not." I'd never heard him sound so stern. "Can't live in the past."

Then he looked at Kitty, and poured himself another gin.

Five years ago, my father died at his desk. Harvey found him. He told the police he stood there for a long time, watching Dad's body grow cold.

"Must have been in shock," he later said. "He was like my shadow."

They even walked alike. The same lilt, a little to the left.

The chainsaw now goes silent. "Nearly done!" Harvey shouts.

Mother and I manage limp waves.

It's thirty-two degrees, officially freezing, and we're getting ready for a Christmas Eve swim. It's Harvey's idea. He and Dad always took a swim in Lake Superior on Christmas when they were kids.

"Fitting way to say good-bye to your dad's lake," he told me. "Don't you think?"

"Never thought about it," I said. "Never thought I'd have to say good-bye."

I feel bad about that now.

Harvey puts the chainsaw down and runs toward us. Puts his arm around me. Gives me a squeeze. "You'll love this," he says. "When you hit that cold water, and your heart stops for just a minute, it'll put the fear of God in you better than church." Then he laughs. It is so cold his teeth rattle like coffee cups.

"Harvey," Mother scolds. "Finish the hole."

"Henpecked," he says to me in mock resignation. Then, like a good boy, he leans over and kisses my mother's forehead and runs back to his work.

"They are just like children," she says. Kitty always says this about men. I want to disagree, but decide against it. This is my last night at Dad's Lake. Next week, it will probably belong to someone else's father. I don't want to argue. That's not why I came. I just want to be here one more time. Just want to stand on this shoreline. Just want a perfect moment at this perfect place. I take another sip of champagne and watch Harvey as he works.

It takes him a while to cut through the ice, but finally the swimming hole is ready for us. My nose is completely numb.

From where I'm standing, close enough to the winding house to make a run for it, I can see that the hole is perfectly round and big enough for all of us. The moonlight is shaky and pale. Harvey inspects the hole carefully. He's wearing an old pair of black galoshes with buckles and a beautiful cashmere coat the color of fawns. The chainsaw is still screaming in one hand. He waves it to the heavens.

"Happy Birthday, Jesus!" he shouts over the din.

Then turns off the chainsaw. He is laughing and panting at the same time. The air reeks of gas and feels close. Steam rises from the hole he's cut into the ice. It's then that it happens. Harvey turns back to us and does something I've never seen him do before: he salutes.

Mother and I stop laughing because at that moment Harvey looks so much like my father it's overwhelming. I can hardly breathe. I can hear Dad's voice again, and imagine him on the Big Boat. All gas and smoke. Creeps into your dreams. Tears roll down my cheeks. I want, so badly, to hear the stories again, to sail the Big Boat with Dad. My mother reaches up and hands me a paper napkin. Her hand is trembling.

"Wipe your face, darling," she says softly.

"It's just the wind," I say.

She takes off her sunglasses. Her eyes are filled with tears, too.

Harvey runs over to us. Mother quickly puts her sunglasses back on. I wipe my face. He doesn't notice we've been crying. "How's my girls?" he says. "Too cold out here for you?"

Then he puts his arm around me and gives me a hug like he used to when I was just a girl and he was still my uncle Harvey. I notice the champagne has turned to slush in my cup.

"It's nearly as bad as incest," my sister said, and threw their wedding invitation in the trash.

"You're being a little hard on them, aren't you?" I asked. Josie hasn't spoken to me since.

She was right, of course. I know that now. But he's still my uncle Harvey. And Kitty is always Kitty. They're all we have.

Still, I don't know why I've come.

"Come on, chickens!" Harvey says, all buttered-rum cheerful. He tosses his cashmere coat across my mother's lap. Underneath the coat, he's wearing Hawaiian-print swimming trunks. Baggy. They catch the night air like twin sails. "I've still got it," he says, and winks. Then poses like the strong man in a sideshow.

He is, indeed, well built for his age. Never been married before. Works out with a trainer. Harvey is what Kitty would call "vital."

"Full of piss and vinegar," Dad used to say.

He and Harvey were in the pyrotechnics business together, specialists in corporate and community events. The plant is right across the border in Wisconsin. A conglomerate from China is currently the highest bidder.

"It doesn't feel the same without your dad," Harvey told me. "He was the brains of this operation. I just did what I was told."

My mother had a different take.

"They were both madmen with dangerous toys."

It's funny, but I remember Dad differently. To me, he was a serious man—not given to toys, or madness. He worked long hours. Always worried about the business. Never left his desk.

"I'll vacation when I die," he'd say.

I am still waiting for his postcard.

Every summer, we took our vacation with Harvey instead. It didn't seem strange at the time. My mother didn't drive, so Harvey was our only hope. Since he designed the shows, there wasn't much for him to do after Independence Day. So every July 18, my birthday, we waved good-bye to my father, jumped into Harvey's Thunderbird convertible, and headed to Florida.

The T-Bird was black with lots of chrome and a candy apple red interior. Kitty, in her cat's-eye sunglasses, sat in front. When we put the top down, her ever-present scarf slapped in the wind like a storm warning.

The first night we'd always stop at Howard Johnson's, where a birthday meant a free sundae to go along with the clam-strip dinner. After dinner was done, we'd go back to our rooms. I'd write my father the first of fourteen letters, one for every day we were gone, on the motel stationery.

"I had an extra scoop for you," I'd always write. "xxxooo."

In all those years of all those vacations—an entire decade of them, to be exact—I never wondered why, at the motels, Kitty always took a separate room, right next to Harvey's. Now that my father's dead, I think about it a lot.

Harvey had the best of us—hot summer days on the shore, birthdays and ice cream. My father had our sickness, our sadness, and the sobbing nights of tornadoes or blizzards—or any number of things that frightened us because they were well beyond our control.

Love is well beyond our control.

Kitty pours champagne in my paper cup. "Would you like some more?" she asks, as if there's a choice.

"Aren't we going for a swim?" Harvey says. "We can drink later."

His smile is crooked, ripples like the lake underneath our feet. He grabs me around the waist, and I can feel his body shaking, mostly from cold. He hugs me as a child would, all sloppy love and need.

"Thanks for coming," he says. "Means a lot."

My champagne is between us. He jostles it by accident, and liquid spills onto the collar of my red wool coat, slides down the strap of my bathing suit. The bubbles leave a trail of goose bumps and ice.

"Sorry," he says, and looks at me with my father's eyes. For a moment, we are breathing the same breath, like horses—all steam and heat.

"I really am sorry," he says, and it is clear that he is not talking about the champagne.

I know that he's sorry. He's sorry about it all, but I say nothing. The moment rusts.

Harvey pulls away, uncomfortable. "Got to go toast up," he says, and runs toward the bonfire before I can see his face, but his tears have fallen on my coat. As he runs his boots jingle like far-off sleigh bells, like somebody else's Christmas.

My mother and I are silent. She pours herself another drink. Most of it, this time, ends up in the cup. She looks out at the freshly cut hole in the ice, the blackness of the water.

"It's hard not to miss him," she says, and squeezes my hand. "The lake house is the last part of him. Hard to see it go."

Creeps into your dreams, I think. I don't know what to say, so we stay like this for a while, not speaking, just listening to the bonfire behind us kick and spit, watching the wind brush snow across the tarnished ice.

After a time, I realize Harvey is standing at the bonfire watching us, and I wonder how we look to him. Like sailors' women waiting. He sees me watching him. Caught, he laughs. Runs past us. "Come on!" he shouts, and runs to the hole in the ice we've been staring at. His "swimming hole," as he calls it. As he runs, his arms are flailing. He nearly trips as his boots slide along the slick lake. He looks like a cartoon, like Elmer Fudd.

I begin to laugh; it's hard not to. He's beet red and flapping. My mother is still holding my hand. I can feel her sweat on my palm when Harvey cannonballs into the water. The lake shoots up like a fountain.

"Harvey truly loves you," she says. "Always has."

I drink the rest of my champagne in one swallow. "You, too," I say, and immediately regret the tone.

Mother lets go of my hand.

In his perfect hole, in the perfectly freezing water, Har-

vey, unaware, is jumping up and down. "Oh, come, all ye
faithful," he sings in a false vibrato, my father's voice. "Joyful
and triumphant! Oh, come ye, oh, come ye to Bethlehem."

I want to run, but he motions us into the water.

"Too cold," Kitty shouts back. She is watching him, un-
smiling.

He begins the song again. "Joyful and triumphant!" he
sings. It's clear he's forgotten the words.

"I'm sorry you and your sister don't approve," Mother
says, angry. Her voice is dark and low.

"It's almost midnight," I say.

She looks at me, terse and thin lipped, expecting another
remark. I'm fresh out, so I take the cup from her hand.

"Better go," I say gently. "Midnight kiss and all that."

She hesitates, then stands, always graceful, always Kitty,
and walks toward him, without a word. Doesn't look back.

I drink the rest of her champagne. It smells of her perfume, of musk and roses. A cloud silts over the moon. I look
at my watch. There's not much time left. It has been agreed
that at midnight there will be fireworks. It's Harvey's idea.

"Just like the old days," he said, meaning the days before
me and Kitty and Josie. The days when he and my father
would shoot bottle rockets into the sky and scream, "Happy
birthday!" Those were the days when they knew each other's
thoughts.

On the other side of the chaise lounge, there's the box
Harvey brought from the office for the occasion. It's red and
yellow, with the names of the rockets in Chinese characters
and English, side by side.

Harvey is still singing while I fumble in my coat pockets for some matches. His voice is clear, rises and falls. I rummage through the box. The names of Chinese fireworks are always so beautiful—"Coconut Grove Song," "Fringed Iris"—as beautiful as the fireworks themselves. The Chinese have a way with pyrotechnics. They transform chemistry into art. Charcoal for the gold sparks. Calcium carbonate for the red stars. Bismuth trioxide for stars that crackle, what they call "Dragon Stars." Barium chlorate for the green flames.

It's all formulas and electrical ignitions. Then beauty. Then hope.

In the bottom of the box, there's a large rocket painted with happy children holding lotus blossoms: "Mountain Flower in Full Bloom." I pull it out and set it on the ice. Nearly two feet tall, it has a long wick. It's a shooter. It'll go far, but could also explode in your face. I kick the rest of the box away from the rocket, just to be careful.

On the shore, the bonfire has made its way through the old doors and now, halfhearted, has settled down, smoldering.

I look at my watch. It's ten seconds to midnight. I kick the chaise lounge away, too. It rattles, frozen. I'm standing over the rocket with my matches.

"Happy birthday," I whisper to the heavens, and look out over the lake.

In the water, Harvey is still jumping up and down, red faced in the moonlight. My mother stands over him on the ice. She seems a little hesitant, not quite ready to take the icy plunge into the "swimming hole." Still, he cajoles her until she takes off her scarf. It trails away, caught in the wind like a cirrus cloud. I strike a match, but I can't stop watching them. Her coyote coat, silver as her hair, silver as the moon, makes her look like an animal. Something large and hungry. Something I've never seen before. She jumps into the water, still wearing the coat.

I light the wick. It hisses.

Harvey has now stopped singing, stopped jumping. He pulls her closer. She screams, joyful, then laughs.

The burning wick fires the rocket.

Kitty's fur coat floats on the surface, spreads out.

The rocket shoots up.

Harvey takes Kitty into his arms, and there's a trail of gold stars.

Kitty places her hand on his face, studies the curve of his nose. Blue stars erupt overhead. She pulls him even closer. Harvey kisses her face, her hair, her lips.

They are floating together in the icy water. Salvaged.

And just when she kisses him back, the rocket explodes into a fountain of stars, all different colors at once—red, violet, gold, and blue.

Chemistry and electricity. Then beauty. Then hope.

◆

The Rules of Engagement

CHLOE FIRMLY BELIEVED "Appomattox is where the South reunited the nation," and this is why Russo had to have her. He had a thing for exotic women. Yet, in all his years of confirmed bachelorhood, he had never once had a southerner. He did, however, have a winter home in Florida.

"Florida is beneath the South," Chloe was quick to point out.

"Well, at Appomattox the South 'reunited' the nation by losing."

This was not going well.

It's not surprising. Chloe was not Russo's usual type. She was, after all, nearly his age. She could speak only one language other than English, and that was Creole French, which she learned during her years at Tulane Law School. She was the type of woman who could be described as voluminous. Her silver hair towered over all like the wedding cake of a wayward bride. She laughed often, loudly. Sometimes she sang at the piano during happy hour. And she liked to drink bourbon, neat.

Chloe showed little interest in Russo, and that encouraged him. She wasn't interested in his collection of vintage automobiles. Nor in his trust fund, his carefully tailored suits, his Mark Twain–inspired silver hair and mustache, his spray-on tan, his ability to write Sanskrit—or how his Melrose-cum-SoHo-inspired mixed-use development would breathe new life into her hometown, "the hurricane-stricken city of Jackson, Mississippi," as the grant said.

Stories about his time spent at Harvard bored her.

"How could you have gone to a school that did not have a real football team?" she asked.

Since Chloe was a southerner, Russo always directed any conversation gone astray back to the Civil War. It seemed to be a topic of interest for her people. After all, they still flew those flags everywhere, still called people like Russo "Yanks." And so he said, "Did you know that Lee surrendered repeatedly? Not just at Appomattox, but at so many other sites that you actually need a car to drive around and see all the places where he shouted, 'I give.' "

Russo meant this as a point of information. Later, upon reflection, he would consider it to be a slight miscalculation on his part. Instead of making Chloe appreciate the scope of Lee's actions, she walked out of the restaurant without another word.

Her sudden departure surprised everyone, since Chloe owned Dupree's, and it was lunch time, and a tour bus filled with ladies from that red and purple book club hat group, which Chloe could never remember the name of, were seated at tables five through nine, all demanding separate checks despite what the sign above them read.

As the door slammed behind Chloe, her son and head chef, Thomas Andrew Jackson Dupree III, shook his mammoth head. "This is not going to end well, Bubba," he said, and took Russo's untouched plate back into the kitchen.

Russo was stricken. He knew that Chloe would eventually think it over, understand that she'd overreacted, and seek his company once more. But the loss of Dupree's lunch special was a painful defeat, and he couldn't exactly go after the plate.

Before Thomas Andrew took up cooking and moved back home to help his mother open the restaurant, he'd been a professional wrestler. His stage name was the Intimidator, and it was a name well earned. He could crush a coconut in one hand, and frequently would, but Thomas Andrew was a poet in the kitchen. Dupree's shrimp and grits were world renowned, talked about on the Food Network. Russo often dreamt of them. The Gulf shrimp were fat and sweet, yet slightly briny. The country ham was as complex as any Prosciutto di Parma hung out to cure under the Italian stars. And so, when the plate was removed, Russo, though he insisted on calling the grits "polenta," nearly wept.

That night, Russo returned to Dupree's. He'd come to say he was sorry, but instead of knocking on the door, he stood on the sidewalk and watched though the large plate-glass window as Chloe closed up. The restaurant was set for the next day's rush; Chloe traveled from table to table, inspecting. She ran a careful hand over each white tablecloth, smoothing the linen. She polished the occasional silver knife or spoon on her silk scarf. Refolded napkins. Adjusted the water glasses so they were perfectly aligned.

Her ivory dress, her silver hair piled high on her head,

her pale pearl skin: *The moon made manifest,* Russo thought and wanted to tell her this, but wasn't sure if he should. The moon is the only planet that man has explored, laid a claim to, planted a flag on, played a round of golf upon. He had already reminded her that the North won the Civil War—that was enough for one day.

When Chloe was finished, she stopped by the cash register, kissed the tips of her fingers lightly, and placed the kiss gently on the large photo of a man that hung there. Until that moment, Russo had seen the photo only as part of the wall. Never really noticed it. Never asked who the "Dupree" of Dupree's was. Never thought twice about it. Didn't even remember what the man looked like, except for the fact that he was wearing a nice suit: blue pinstriped, double-breasted.

But the kiss said everything: it said "husband."

Chloe turned off the lights, came out the door, and stopped. "I'm tired," she said. "Just go away."

Russo could smell the scent of gardenias, or maybe he just thought he did.

For a moment, they stood looking at each other with a loss for words. The street was deserted; it was well past midnight. The pink light from the streetlamp above them softened the lines in their faces, made them seem younger to each other, as if they had met before the husband, before the children, before the strings of failed affairs.

"The war is over," Russo said, but wasn't sure what war he really meant.

She turned and walked away.

After that, Russo was determined to prove to Chloe that

she'd misjudged him. Just because he came from the north—
St. Paul, Minnesota, a town more Irish than northern in a
Civil War kind of way—that didn't mean he was any less a
gentleman than someone who was born below the Mason-
Dixon Line. After all, he had hair like Mark Twain and even
a white suit—that should count for something.

The next day, he stepped into an antique store and
bought a silver-handled walking stick that he'd admired in
the window. "A gentleman's furnishing," the dealer told him.

"Perfect," he said.

And then he began to steal the silverware from Dupree's.

This was part of his plan—a bold plan, even by his own
admission. Every day that Chloe would not speak to him,
Russo took a little something. He thought of each bit as a
piece of her heart. As soon as he slipped the first iced tea
spoon into his pocket, he knew it was a gallant gesture that
bespoke a great longing. He knew he loved her.

Unfortunately, Russo loved all women—many of them at
the same time.

He couldn't help himself. Something about the way they
rear-ended him at a stoplight, or sued him for shoddy con-
struction practices—even just the sound of the door slam-
ming behind them—made him love them even more.

Russo loved women so very much that one gave him a
daughter—quite literally. On her eighth birthday, Alana was
deposited at Russo's door.

"Surprise," Alana said. "She didn't want me, either."

The girl was gangly and almond skinned: a product of a
one-night stand with a cocktail waitress on the island of

Kona. Her mother, Makaha (*Mah' kah hah*), which means "fierce"—a fact Russo wished he'd known before he'd arranged to meet her after her shift—lived in the old ways. About the time Makaha met Russo, she'd just denied her American citizenship and joined the yet-to-be-formed independent nation of Hawaii, with different laws, no democracy, and no connection to the U.S. Constitution or justice system.

Unfortunately, Makaha also had no tolerance for margaritas. And so, when Alana was born, she sued Russo for child support and wouldn't allow him visitation rights.

"You are the conqueror," she told him.

Russo sort of liked the sound of that.

Eight years later, Makaha and the rest of her group, the Kingdom of Hawaiian Trust, stormed the Iolani Palace in Honolulu. The 1882 palace, once the home of King Kalakaua, had been converted into a museum and was clogged with swarms of tourists wearing "I ♥ Hawaii" T-shirts.

The separatists were not deterred. They locked the gates, declared ownership, announced that they had the right to serve as the island's legitimate government, and attempted to sit their own self-declared king on King Kalakaua's throne and then secede from the United States.

Unfortunately, while an interesting plan, their "king" had never been to the palace before. None of the group had. So no one, except the tour guides and tourists, had any idea where the throne was—and the tour guides and tourists weren't telling.

It was a tense standoff. A pink-skinned woman from New Jersey kept screaming, "What is this? Some theater show like *Tony and Tina's Wedding*?" After an hour of this, Makaha and the Kingdom of Hawaiian Trust surrendered. The "king" was arrested. Makaha was arrested. Child services stepped in, and Russo suddenly became a father.

Alana lived up to her name, which means "awakening."

She taught Russo how to wash dishes, buy groceries, and bowl. He taught her the ancient art of Japanese scroll painting, but she took up basketball instead.

Happiness became microwaved macaroni and cheese and Saturday morning cartoons. Every year, even through high school, they'd send a Christmas card with their photos. Neither could decide who would be the elf, so the two of them both dressed as Santa. Alana always winked at the camera. The older she grew, the more the wink worried Russo.

Then she left for Harvard. Just like that. Russo felt no sense of pride, just loneliness. He spent most nights on the posh end of Summit Avenue at the University Club. Its high ceilings, dark wood dining rooms, and wood-burning fireplace reminded him of his own Harvard days. He sat at the bar drinking martinis and watching the silent television, the strangers around him providing the soundtrack. And then came Katrina. And opportunity. And so he came to Jackson. And then to Dupree's.

When Russo met Chloe, he was a little out of practice; he hadn't actually dated in over a decade. Still, he proved to be an industrious man, especially when it came to acquiring various items from the Reed & Barton Country French hotel series collection. At the end of one month, he'd "liberated" (a term he preferred) twenty-one salad forks, seven teaspoons, twelve iced tea spoons, one butter knife, and two seafood forks. He also had in his possession three dozen Premier all-Murata air-jet-spun dinner napkins in winter white. And a honey dispenser.

It was $568 worth of Chloe's 5 percent profit margin.

Russo was amazed at how easy it was. No one seemed to bother him. He entered Dupree's every night at 6:30 PM, and a member of the staff, not Chloe, sat him. As per his usual, he looked at the menu but ordered whatever special Thomas Andrew Jackson Dupree III had to offer: a bourbon-grilled tenderloin topped with Vidalia onion slivers, a country trout finished with red pepper and chive oils, medallions of pork served with freshly made peach chutney and drizzled with a savory beurre blanc—it was all magical. There were starters of local chèvre cheesecake and sweet smoked Louisiana oysters. Desserts of Meyer lemon custard and thin brown sugar tarts.

While he ate his meal, he avoided looking at the large photo of Mr. Thomas Andrew Jackson Dupree II that hung over the register.

Every night, Chloe made her rounds at all the tables except his. Russo could hear her laugh, her scold, her tease and cajole everyone around him. He'd drink his wine until the bottle was gone, and bit by bit the silverware, napkins, and honey dispenser became his.

But Chloe did not.

On the fourth Friday of Russo's exile, he came in for lunch. Chloe didn't go back into the kitchen when he arrived. She stopped him at the door.

"Do you know how to make waffles?" she asked.

Russo suspected that the word *waffles* was a code of some sort—as in, "If I sleep with you on Saturday, will you make waffles for me on Sunday morning?" He found himself blushing—and at a loss for words.

"Never mind," she said and sat him near the kitchen at a small wobbly two top. Still, Russo was happy. Progress was being made.

That day he eyed a steak knife and a long-stemmed French-style Cabernet Sauvignon balloon glass. But they remained. Chloe had, after all, finally spoken to him. It didn't seem right to take anything else.

On his way out, she invited him into her office.

"Am I here to discuss waffles?" he said. Russo was prepared. He handed her a business card with the address of his rented town house written on the back. "I have an excellent waffle maker. Vintage, but still top of the line." And then he winked.

Russo liked euphemisms. Chloe, apparently, did not.

"Mr. Russo," she said, with a chill in her voice that Russo guessed could ice a Sancerre in under thirty seconds, "here's what's going to happen. You will write a check for all the things you've taken in the past thirty days, or return them."

He wasn't quite sure he heard right. "But what about waffles? I thought we were going to talk about my waffles."

Chloe seemed embarrassed. "At first, I thought, perhaps,

well, maybe you needed the money, and since one of the line cooks for Sunday brunch just quit . . ."

"I don't understand."

"I know. You don't have a clue. And Thomas Andrew finds that annoying. And when Thomas Andrew is annoyed, things begin to happen. Bad things. So I would rather just take a check. That would be better for all concerned. Safer for you, in particular."

Russo had never been accused of stealing before. He felt dizzy, flushed. "Who could possibly say that I would do such a thing?"

Thomas Andrew was the first name that came to Russo's mind, but Chloe pointed at a small security camera mounted in the corner. It was painted white, like the ceiling, and very difficult to see. Russo opened the office door and looked out over the dining room. He counted at least four more.

So Russo did the only thing he could do: he left without a word. Slammed the office door behind him. He would not pay for the items he had "liberated," nor would he return them. It was a matter of principle. People take things all the time from restaurants; everyone knows it's built into the price. Butter, crackers, salt and pepper shakers—if it's on the table, it's offered to you, part of the hospitality.

Any real southern woman would know that, he thought, but yet, strangely, still wanted her. And so he vowed that as Union commander Ulysses S. Grant conquered the South, so would he.

Unfortunately, history was not Russo's strongest subject

at Harvard. Yes, Grant did accept the South's surrender, but he hardly won. The South did not go down easily. Some say it never went down at all.

But Chloe's skin smelled of vanilla, and her eyes were, indeed, the color of bourbon, and somehow the sound of her voice made him happy. And so he would have her.

The "how" of the situation was just a minor detail, and Russo never worried about details. He was, as he often referred to himself, "a big-picture man." Which, in retrospect, seemed odd because it was a very small detail that brought him to post-Katrina Jackson, Mississippi, in the first place.

Hot air. Or, more precisely, the lack of it.

Right before Katrina hit Jackson, the city was declared a disaster area. It was an unusual move by the federal government, but Katrina was an unusual storm. They were expecting the worst, but before the hurricane reached the state capital, its towering thunderclouds, its "hot towers," dissipated.

So when the hurricane arrived—no hot air. No overcooked winds. When Katrina rolled into Jackson, she'd topped out at 47 MPH, gusts of 74 MPH. They'd seen worse from tornados. Not more than sixty houses were damaged enough to be declared uninhabitable, and most of that was roof damage. But to the federal government, this was just a detail. Red Cross and FEMA money flowed into Jackson— and so did Russo.

And so after lunch, and the unfortunate misunderstanding over his "liberation" of Chloe's cutlery, Russo met with his project manager to discuss even more new avenues for

FEMA funding. On the way to the meeting, he sang along with the radio, "money for nothin' and your chicks for free," because he knew that Chloe would understand her breach of etiquette and ask his forgiveness. And he would forgive her. And have her. She was his for the taking.

She was speaking to him, after all. She, indeed, would be his.

It was no surprise when Russo arrived home after his meeting and saw Chloe dressed in a lovely peach silk dress, sitting, as he knew southern women are likely to do, on the porch swing.

For a moment, Russo stood on the sidewalk watching her, his weight carefully balanced on his antique silver-handled cane. He wanted to give her the full effect of his gentlemanly air, and wished he'd bought a white Panama hat. *This would be a good time to tip one,* he thought, *a courtly gesture.*

"Good afternoon," he said, and nodded. "You look serene."

In actuality, she did not. Russo had failed to notice that the front window of his house was broken and that Chloe had at her feet a box of $568 worth of the Reed & Barton Country French hotel series collection, three dozen dinner napkins, and a honey dispenser.

Russo's big-picture mentality had failed him again.

Chloe did not smile. She handed him a check for $75. "For the window," she said. "I called AAA 24-Hour Window Replacement. They're on their way. Ten minutes or so." Then she picked up the box and started to leave. Russo caught her by the arm.

"Why don't we call a truce?"

"In a truce, one understands the other."

"We could talk about it over a glass of wine."

"Why did I come back to Jackson?"

"Money?"

She began to walk away.

Russo called after her. "I have a daughter."

Chloe didn't turn around. "How do I know you're not lying?"

Russo suddenly felt a pain in his chest. "Because I miss her," he said, and Chloe could hear it in his voice. He flipped opened his cell phone with the latest Christmas photo—he and Alana dressed in ill-fitting Santa suits, both winking at the camera. He held it out to her.

Chloe studied the photo carefully. "She's very pretty."

"Her mother was Hawaiian," he said. "And smart enough to not want me."

Chloe smiled for the first time in a long time.

Russo tossed his gentleman's cane through the open window. It rattled onto the wood floors. He rolled up his jacket and tossed it in, too. "Here," he said, "let me take these to your car."

Russo took the box, looked inside. All those pieces of silver he'd so proudly culled looked tarnished, like something you'd pick up at a garage sale. A box of junk, worthless except to the person who actually owned it—and that clearly was not him.

"I'm sorry," he said. "I wasn't thinking."

In the distance, the ambulance that is always racing

somewhere whooped and whined. Like the good Catholic girl she once was, Chloe made the sign of the cross and mumbled a prayer for the fallen. Russo hoped she said one for him, too.

"Homesick," Chloe said. "After Andy died, I came back because I missed this place. We were grade school sweethearts; we grew up here, married here."

He felt her sadness as if it were his own, and so he said, "What the heart has once owned and had, it shall never lose."

Then Russo reached out and touched her on the arm, as a friend would: a moment of comfort.

"That's beautiful. I'll remember that."

"It was Henry Ward Beecher," Russo said without thinking. "Abolitionist. Brother of *Uncle Tom's Cabin*'s Harriet Beecher Stowe."

And this was the truth—much to Russo's horror. *How could I have forgotten that?* What's worse, Beecher led his own volunteer infantry against the South. Russo was hoping beyond hope that Chloe didn't know that.

"We're back to the Civil War?" she sighed, giving the word *war* three syllables instead of one. "And you tell me southerners are obsessed."

I'm losing her, Russo thought. *Again.*

"Of course," he said. "Beecher also advocated keeping the poor as poor as possible. He told a group of starving workers, 'If you are being reduced, go down boldly into poverty.' And then he left for a two-month vacation in Europe.

"So generally speaking he was sort of an idiot—but he got lucky every now and then."

"Like you?"

He shrugged. They stood with the box of silverware between them.

"You really are not very smooth with the ladies, are you?"

He shook the box slightly. "This is *not* smooth?"

She laughed and then leaned over the $568 worth of stolen merchandise and kissed him. Quickly. "Don't get any ideas. I just wanted to see what that was like."

Russo's ears felt hot. "And?"

"What time is it?"

He looked at his watch, nearly dropped the box. "3:20 PM."

"Come on."

Chloe took the silverware and started back down the sidewalk.

"What about the window?" he called after her, but she didn't turn around. She opened the trunk of a new black Mercedes SLK, placed the box inside, and got in.

He had no idea that was her car. Suddenly it occurred to him that she was right. He knew nothing about her at all.

"Are you coming?" she asked.

Russo was.

They drove along in silence. Her silver hair took on the colors of the Delta sun, flared and sparked. Just outside of Jackson, Chloe turned onto an unmarked dirt road.

"How about dinner?" Russo asked.

"Thomas Andrew found someone who can handle the rush."

Russo meant his own dinner, as in *their* dinner—together. That's where he assumed they were going. Someplace out of town. Romantic. Secluded. Away from Thomas Andrew. But before Russo could clarify, Chloe took a sharp turn and pulled into a clearing, a makeshift parking lot. Up ahead, there was some sort of an encampment: a large tent and several other smaller ones off to each side. A hand-painted banner read, "The 46th Mississippi Infantry."

Something must be burning, he thought. Everything was cloaked in a haze of smoke, hardly seemed real. There was the dark, acid smell of gunpowder. Above it all flew a series of flags—including the Southern Cross.

Chloe drove up to a sign that read, "Drop-off. No Parking," put the car in park, and turned to Russo. "If you want to know my heart, here it is," she said.

Russo was unsure of what to do. He wanted to kiss her again—she looked so beautiful sitting there—and yet, at the same time, *Klan,* he thought. *It's a Klan thing.* He checked his watch again. 3:45. The sun was waning. He could see that the woods would soon be dark, the kind of deep-woods darkness that humbles.

"This is Thomas Andrew's infantry," she said.

Makes sense. Russo imagined the towering chef wearing a Premier all-Murata air-jet-spun tablecloth in winter white with two eyeholes cut out and a conical colander on his head to provide the point of the hood.

But then—gunfire. Russo jumped. It was close, too close. And not like the kind you hear on television, but a fist-in-the-gut sort of sound: a series of booms. Then more smoke, then screaming.

Russo flipped open his phone. Alana, dressed as Santa, was still winking.

"History is all just numbers until you see it up close," Chloe said. "Just take the path into the clearing."

Russo did not like the sound of this.

"Thomas Andrew will bring you home."

He liked this even less. But she was so beautiful. And now speaking to him again. And kissing him. *This Klan thing could just be a phase*, he thought.

Russo opened the car door, and a voice boomed from a scratchy PA system, "In His name we shall cast out these devils; they who were once our own now speak with new tongues, take up with serpents!"

Chloe looked up at him with those bourbon eyes, opened the glove compartment, and handed him a small white flag. "You'll need this. Keep your head low."

Then she drove away.

The smell of wood smoke made the air feel heavy, clouded the sky. Russo flipped open his cell phone. No bars. No reception—just Alana and her wink. Thomas Andrew was his only way to get home again. So he walked up the path dangling the flag in front of him. "Switzerland!" he shouted, because he didn't know what else to say.

It didn't matter. The gunfire drowned him out. And then a cannon's boom. Then an explosion. A fireball shot up, like a fountain, from the center of the encampment. The pain in Russo's chest grew tighter. "Switzerland! Switzerland!"

Over the loudspeaker, the voice came again. "We are surrounded."

Fear is an efficient motivator. Russo didn't know which way to run, so he just ran forward, full speed, head down, into the tent, screaming, "Switzerland!"

And then fell over.

Everyone turned to look at him, even those lying on the ground. Yankees, Confederates: their bodies were stacked like matchsticks, but at the sight of the screaming man in modern dress, they sat up, leaned on their elbows. Women and children, dressed in hoopskirts and flour-sack shirts, stopped praying over their kin and looked at him, too. Even the horses stared.

White faced, sweating, flag in hand: "Switzerland," Russo said again, but this time he was nearly whispering. His Mark Twain hair gave him a wild, misguided look.

Thomas Andrew, dressed as his great-grandfather, a Confederate cavalry officer, got up from being dead and jogged across the field. "Sorry, guys!" he was shouting. Waving his sword. "Sorry!"

He helped Russo up off the ground "This is a closed drill. Next month. The Spring Campaign is next month. Not now."

Russo was dizzy. "Your mother kissed me."

Thomas Andrew paused, shook his head. "Bubba, I told you no good would come of this."

Russo looked around. "This . . ." he was searching for the word. *Klan gathering* was all he could think of. "This . . ."

". . . reenactment."

Russo nodded, relieved. "So it's not a . . ."

"It's funded by the state historical society."

"Your mother said her heart was here."

Thomas Andrew smiled. Put his mammoth arm around the man. For a moment, Russo was worried he'd be crushed. "All our hearts are here. Abandoned. When you know your kin had to stand a foot away from a man, look into his eyes, and pull the trigger—that kind of killing leaves a stain that time can't heal."

Russo thought about this for a moment. "How many?"

"Seven hundred thousand. More than any war before or since."

Russo didn't know what to say. He suddenly felt cold. Started to shake.

Thomas Andrew took off his mammoth gray topcoat and put it around Russo's shoulders. Adjusted the epaulets. It dwarfed him. "You look like you need a drink."

The rehearsal was over, and so the two men sat by the bonfire under the Southern Cross and drank bourbon until night fell, and then some. They talked about nothing in particular—football, women but not Chloe, the Delta, and the exquisite fleeting beauty of a goat cheese soufflé and a well-made bowl of macaroni and cheese. And they drank until they were quite drunk, and then some.

◆

We Are All Just Visitors Here

OUTSIDE THE POOL CAGE, a small green snake is making its way through the spiky grass. The sun is high, hot. The snake and the grass are nearly the same color, a grayish green. Both shimmer in the heat. The sun is so bright that Jim has to squint to see the snake as it slinks through the blades of grass, all tongue and ink eyes. "Your fault," he says to the snake. The snake moves along, uncaring.

Overhead, the Thunderbirds practice for their next air show. The air force base isn't far from Laguna Shores, the golf community where Jim and his wife live, just a couple of miles or so. The only *laguna* in Laguna Shores is on the fourth hole. Sand traps and small alligators surround it. It has a plastic lining, no coral. The Thunderbirds practice every Monday from 1200 to 1245 hours. Swoop low over the manicured grass. The F-16s braid exhaust, rattle and boom. Cause waves.

It is a lucky thing that snakes are deaf, Jim thinks. He's deaf himself, ever since Vietnam. The planes rattle his bones. With both hearing aids off, he only feels the sound, doesn't hear it. Just like the water in the pool, Jim shakes.

It's not so bad being deaf, he tells himself. It has its advantages, especially every Monday from 1200 to 1245 hours.

"Thunderbird time"—that's what he and his wife call it. Of course, Jim and Maureen are usually never home during practice. Today's the exception.

The snake stops for a moment and rises up as if it's heard something. Its head scans the horizon. Maybe for food, Jim thinks, or blue heron. Herons eat snakes. Jim's seen them slurp snakes down like spaghetti. Maybe that snake thinks he hears a heron.

"It's just the ghosts singing," Jim says as if to reassure the reptile. Talking to snakes is a habit Jim's gotten into recently. Laguna Shores is filled with them. Some are poisonous, some not. Snakes are always a problem in these developments. When you disturb their natural habitat, it forces them to live places they would not normally choose to—like a $500,000, three-bedroom, Venetian-styled pool home complete with outdoor spa. So snakes can often be seen wandering the golf course, deaf and confused. Sometimes striking out at people, just because.

Jim feels a certain kinship to them.

"I get that ghost singing, too," he tells this one. "Just your mind playing tricks."

The doctor has told Jim that what he calls "ghosts singing" is an "auricular episode of the inner ear." That's just a fancy name for phantom sounds that are lodged in the memory and play back for no apparent reason. "It's spooky," Jim told his wife. "Sounds real, but it's just a trick."

Sometimes it's a roaring, like the surf. Or a clanging, like church bells. But, just recently, he's been hearing a whistle, soft and low, like a man calling a dog during the hunt. That really spooks him.

Back when Jim was a kid, his father used to whistle for their dog, Rocket, like that. It's illegal to hunt with dogs, but Jim's dad didn't care. He used to tell Jim, "My property. My dog. My business. This is still America—don't you forget that."

So Jim never did.

Back then, when his father would whistle, the black Lab would run full out into the woods and scatter the deer. Made for easy prey. Jim still remembers the way his rifle would kick and a buck would rise up on its hind legs, reel with surprise, and then fall. Or, sometimes, it would just run, confused, until the dying took hold.

When Jim hears that particular bit of ghost music, the forgotten rumble of his father's whistle, it all comes back to him. He can feel the heat of the buck slit open, and feel its eyes on him. The eyes—he really doesn't want to think about them. So the whistle has become a problem.

He'd like to tell Maureen about this because it would explain everything and she'd forgive him. But he can't because then he'd have to tell her about Phu Hoa Dong. And that would scare her. It still scares him. He'd have to tell her about the bone-aching damp of the foxholes and the stench—that odd mix of swamp air, mud, and vomit. And the constant darkness caused by silos of rotted rice burning. And the rubber trees where the vc would pick you off while you tried to take a piss—but of course Jim wouldn't say "piss." Maybe "piddle" or "tinkle." He'd use a word that wouldn't make Maureen cringe.

"That's why I don't eat rice," he'd like to tell her, and explain that's why he won't go to the Lotus, that new place down the street, even though Maureen assures him they serve American food, too. They have a $5.95 lunch special, she says. And he knows that's true because that's what they've painted across the window. You can read it as you drive by.

"Best soup in town!"

That's painted there, too.

"They must really be a healthy people," Maureen said when the place first opened. "Some of the other girls went, and told me they have big bowls of homemade broth with rice noodles and shrimp and crab and you squeeze lime into it and put fresh mint and basil on top. It just sounds so good, doesn't it? So healthy."

"Sure," Jim said. "We'll give it a try."

But they never do. They can't. It's the rice that stops him. The rice makes him remember. Jim wants to explain that. It's like the whistle. Rice triggers something inside that makes him feel like his arm did after the rifle kicked—that shake after the shot.

Except it's not just my arm, he wants to say, it's everything. Everything shakes. The whole world. Even you.

But he doesn't say this. He can't. He's not sure why. He knows Maureen would understand and feel sorry for him, and they could go back to the way it was. Still, it just doesn't seem like the kind of thing you'd tell another person. Jim's not sure how it would sound if he said all that aloud. So he says nothing.

And now he's standing in the shallow end of the pool with all of his clothes on.

And he knows this is not a particularly good turn of events.

Jim's golf shirt wicks blue water. Without sunscreen, his nose is slowly turning pink, as are the tips of his ears and the soft round spot on his balding head. His belly bobs. His leather wallet feels like a stone in the pocket of his shorts. He takes it out and places it on the pool's edge. Then takes off his boat shoes and shakes the water out of each one. Neatly, he lines them up along the edge of the pool, next to the wallet. Order is good, he thinks. Order must be maintained.

"Maureen?"

She doesn't turn around.

Maureen's standing with her back to him in the deep end. The airplanes overhead slip in and out of the sound barrier, make the water quiver beneath her chin. She's wearing her favorite blue swimsuit. It's flattering, makes her look girlish. Not sixty-two. It's a shame she's still crying. Jim can tell, because he can see her shoulders shake.

That's why he's standing in the pool. He's waiting for her to finish. He's been waiting so long he can feel the tips of his ears burn. He imagines them blistering like fried pork rinds.

Pork rinds.

Now he's made himself hungry.

"Pork rinds and a beer: wouldn't that be tasty right about now?" he says, or thinks he says. It's hard to tell. Jim's feeling a little dizzy, maybe sunstroke. He knows he should have had more than that doughnut for breakfast.

"Maureen?"

She doesn't move.

Jim's tempted to skim his wet wallet across the water, just to get her attention, just to say he's sorry again, but doesn't. He's not a very good shot and therefore the action could be misinterpreted. So he stands with his arms folded, waiting, watching the snake. Jim's never been in the pool with all his clothes on before. His underwear blooms like a jellyfish. He's not sure he likes that.

Unaware of Jim's plight, the snake continues through the grass. Arches like a whip. Probably hisses, Jim thinks. A Wandering Garter, *Thamnophis elegans vagrans*. An elegant vagrant.

Jim's made a study of snakes and dogs and airplanes and movie stars of the 1930s and so many other things that he feels as if he's a walking *Encyclopedia Britannica,* which he's not even sure they print anymore. There's just too much information to remember these days, but he tries anyway. He has to. Jim does crossword puzzles. He studies all sorts of things that can neatly fit into numbered boxes, both up and down. He likes the surety. The word is either right, or not. No gray area.

"I am brilliant in boxes," he tells Maureen. She used to smile when he said that. Seems like a long time ago.

Unfortunately, being "brilliant in boxes" doesn't come in handy when you're standing in a swimming pool fully dressed.

Jim puts his hand to his lips. "Honey?"

He knows he said that for sure; he could feel his breath run across his fingers.

"How about some pork rinds?"

Jim checks his watch. It's 12:32 PM, well past lunch. He figures Maureen has been crying in the swimming pool for about fifteen minutes, more or less. Before she got into the pool, she was crying in the bedroom. Before that, she was crying in the emergency room. All in all, Jim figures, just off the top of his head, Maureen's been crying for the better part of two hours and forty-five minutes.

He'd like her to stop, but he's beginning to believe that just isn't possible.

"Want to go shopping?" he shouts. The word *shopping* is usually magic. Jim hates shopping, but would willingly go, right now, soaking wet, if Maureen would just stop crying.

He shouts even louder, or hopes he does. "We could buy a sweater."

Jim is shouting so loudly his voice cracks, but he can't hear it. Of course, neither can Maureen. The fighters overhead are doing figure eights.

"A nice, thick wool one."

No response. Jim looks into the sky and sees blurs of red, white, and blue. It doesn't make him feel patriotic, just frustrated. It's ninety-two degrees, but he knows that if Maureen could hear the word *sweater*, it could change everything. A wool sweater is the one thing Maureen wants more than anything. They have no serious sweaters anymore, just flimsy cotton pastel things that match their golf shorts. And a couple of sweatshirts. They threw all of their winter clothes away when they moved to Florida—that's why Maureen wants one. It's the first step. After the sweater, there'll be a coat. One for her. Then one for him. Pretty soon, they'll be on a plane back to Minneapolis for Christmas.

"Back home," she keeps telling him. Gets that look. "Don't you want to go home?"

Jim knows he can't go back to Minneapolis. Not at Christmas. Not at the Fourth of July. Not ever, even though he misses the life he had there.

"I have also been displaced from my natural habitat," he tells the snakes. And he has.

For twenty-five years, Jim was the executive director at the Center for Deafness, helping others like him. He knew he wasn't ready to retire, but felt he had to. He had to get away.

"Personal reasons," he told the board of directors. He wouldn't elaborate. They just wouldn't understand. Unless you've been to war, it's difficult to explain.

Now, Minneapolis has become Oz to him. The things Jim misses create a hole in him that golf can't heal. It's not just about his job, the sense of purpose it gave him, but odd things like the smell of wood smoke and wet wool. He misses their yearly visit to the state fair, with its deep-fried battered cheese curds—"gut-bombs," Maureen would call them. And it's difficult not to miss the art show in the Agriculture Building, featuring portraits of Elvis, Nixon, and that singer Madonna—and the real Madonna, too—made entirely of sunflower seeds, grits, and wild rice. He misses funny stuff like that. Things that meant home to him, like creamed herring, warm potato *lefse* rolled with sugar at Christmas, and canoeing on the city lakes.

Most of all, Jim misses snowstorms—the way they shut everything down. Their particular silence made him feel less alone.

Jim misses the texture of what his life once was. His "natural habitat," as he says.

"But things change"—that's what he tells the snakes. That's what he tells Maureen every time she talks about going back.

"You should work on your golf swing," he tells her.

So she does, and doesn't speak to him for days on end.

The real problem is Sue-Sue, their grandchild. She's adopted. She's why they left Minneapolis. Sue-Sue is Korean, and that confuses Jim.

To Jim, Sue-Sue looks like a "Charlie," a "Chuck"—Vietcong. He hates these words when he thinks them about an eggshell of a girl, his granddaughter. They're words from another life, a life he thought he'd put behind him. Of course, now he knows better. You can leave a war, but it never leaves you. It stays forever. Tangles up in your heart.

The problem is that Sue-Sue makes him dream. That's when he first heard the ghost whistle, his father's whistle— in a dream.

Jim knows he can work through it, though. He just needs a little distance. But Sue-Sue is their only grandchild, and it's been four years since the adoption, and things haven't gotten that much better. It's tough on Maureen, and Jim knows it. He can hear it in her voice—which strikes him as odd because he can't hear his own voice very well anymore. When he speaks, especially recently, his voice just seems to fade away. Trails off.

Jim has talked to his doctors about this, and they've run lots of tests and found nothing wrong. So Jim has stopped bringing it up. He doesn't want to seem like a complainer. With his new set of digital hearing aids, state of the art, he can hear pretty well. Nearly as good as he used to. He can go to baseball games. Watch TV. He can hear every word the minister says in church. But he can't really hear himself. No big deal, he thinks. I got the whole world to listen to. I'm a lucky man.

So most nights Jim goes to sleep thinking about the moments of his life in which he felt lucky, like his wedding. When he married Maureen she had such a tiny waist he could put his hands around her and his fingers nearly met. It was after the war, but she married him anyway—despite everything.

"I promised, didn't I?" she said, and then signed the word *forever*. Maureen learned sign language as soon as she received the chaplain's letter. The gesture brought tears to Jim's eyes. He'd never been so happy in his life.

Of course now, since Sue-Sue arrived, he understands how difficult the word *forever* can be.

Still, on good nights, he counts that moment, and all the rest, like sheep.

On bad nights, Sue-Sue nights, his dreams shift. He's waist deep in mud and shooting at shadows. He kicks and screams until the moment when, in his dream, he enters the village again, and the child runs toward him laughing, glistening with sweat, and holds out the grenade to him as if it were a mango.

The gun in his hand kicks. He can feel it shake his body. The girl's eyes are a doe's.

He doesn't remember the explosion.

He's never told anyone this part of the story, not even Maureen. It just doesn't seem like something you talk about. Not in proper company.

Now, it feels too late.

Mike, Jim's son, adopted Sue-Sue on her first birthday. The agency sent her to her new home with a dress and a tiny jacket from Korea. "It's a *hanbok,*" the card explained.

"It's a tradition," Mike told his father. "It's important that Sue-Sue understands her heritage."

Jim and Maureen were invited for cake.

Dressed in the *hanbok,* Sue-Sue made her entrance, as all toddlers do, one tentative step after another. The dress was raw silk, pure white, with white embroidered flowers. It was styled like a ball gown, floor-length with clean lines. The tiny jacket shimmered like pearls, like the shells of oysters.

"Like the moon dreaming itself," the card read.

"Doesn't she look beautiful?" Mike said. "In Korea, all the children wear them on their first birthday."

"She looks like a ghost," Jim said, and poured another drink.

That night he heard the ghosts singing, that rumble whistle of his father. And then the dreams began.

Now, overhead, the Thunderbirds circle one another. Practice is nearly over. Jim once read that the planes travel at speeds of 1,000 MPH, or more. The strange thing about them is that when they break the sound barrier you see them do it, but then they're gone. Then you hear the *boom*. Like thunder on a clear day. It's an odd disconnect.

Even odder is the fact that the pilots fly with their knees. It's called the fly-by-wire system. Electrical wires relay commands, replace cable and linkage controls. The air force says it's more accurate during high g-force maneuvers. The pilots lean against a side-stick controller. They lean because the gravity is too strong for them to pull back a center stick.

It's an amazing system, but isn't foolproof, as Jim and his neighbors now know.

Last year there was a midair collision over Laguna Shores, bits of fuselage rained down over everything. It was very impressive, made NBC's *Nightly News*. The pilots ejected safely with just a few broken bones and concussions. One had a ruptured spleen. But they were lucky. The jets were not. Parts burned and fell to the ground in a ten-mile path. One of the fuel tanks started the golf course on fire. Jim's next-door neighbors, Jack and Linda, had a wheel crash through their lanai and land in the hot tub, where Jack was trying out his new prescription of Viagra with the housekeeper.

The rescue team was on the scene within minutes, as was most of the neighborhood. Linda hasn't been seen at the club since. Their lanai still leans a little to the left.

Maureen wants to move, but knows they can't afford it.

So she doesn't push the issue, but Jim knows it's a problem.
It's always been a problem.

"They fly with their knees?" she said, aghast, when they
first toured the development. Right then Jim knew he
shouldn't have told her. So they compromised. Now, every
Monday when the Thunderbirds are in town, between 1200
and 1245 hours, "Thunderbird time," Jim and Maureen always go to lunch. She usually takes the family photo album
with them, and a small silk bag filled with her grandmother's
pearls—just in case there's another accident.

"They fly with their knees," she tells anyone who asks
why she's brought these things.

Right now, Jim would give everything to hear her say that
again, hear her say anything at all. Above the pool, in the jet-
plaid sky, the airplanes bank away. Jim feels their sonic
booms rattle through him as if he were a tuning fork. Then
the moment passes.

"This is ridiculous," he shouts, and knows he is shouting
because he can feel his heart beat faster. "We can't stand in
the pool forever."

Maureen turns around and is clearly still angry. Her eyes
are red and swollen. "I can," she says. "You're leaving."

With his hearing aids off, it takes Jim a minute to read her
lips. He's not sure he's heard right. He turns on his hearing
aids again.

"Where would I go?" he says.

"She's just five years old, for God's sake. What were you
thinking?"

"I wasn't."

Now he's made it even worse, he can tell. Maureen dives underwater, swims farther away from him. Jim turns his hearing aids off again; he's heard enough. He feels as if he's trapped in g-forces and flying with his knees. He's already told everyone he's sorry, he didn't mean to hurt Sue-Sue. It just happened. Just like most of his life. It was an accident, but nobody seems to believe him. Jim suspects they've been waiting for something like this to happen for a long time. He certainly has.

Every year, Sue-Sue, Mike, and his wife, Amy, come to visit for a weekend. This was their weekend. They flew in on Saturday morning and planned to leave Monday night. Things seemed to be going pretty well. As usual, the guest room was filled with their things: mismatched suitcases, wet bathing suits, and baby powder. Maureen cooked meat loaf and mashed potatoes, even though it's too hot to eat such heavy food, but everybody did because they're Mike's favorites. She baked dozens of cookies and packed them with bubble wrap "for the trip home," as she always does.

She even taught Sue-Sue several Broadway show tunes. Maureen has always had a beautiful voice. Before she married Jim, she'd hoped to sing on Broadway. In 1960, she'd auditioned for a revival of *Camelot*. She was called back three times for the part of Lady Anne, but didn't make the final cut.

And then Jim came home—and sign language became more important than song lyrics.

Now she just sings for fun. But when Jim's not around, she sings as if the Majestic is filled and Robert Goulet is about to take the stage.

"You sing pretty, Grammy," Sue-Sue told her.

"Shh," Maureen whispered, "that's a secret."

And it remained one. The entire weekend Jim worked on his golf swing.

Everything was fine until Maureen had an idea.

"Why don't you take Sue-Sue for a ride on the golf cart. She'd like that," she said.

Jim and Maureen were lying in bed talking. It was early, before sunrise. Jim liked to listen to the sound of her voice in the quiet of morning. He had his arms around her waist, her still tiny waist. Just holding her. Feeling her breathe. Everything felt safe. But still Jim hesitated.

Maureen kissed him gently. "Vietnam was a long time ago," she whispered. "A different lifetime. Besides, Sue-Sue is Korean, or was. Now she is an American. Our granddaughter. Our family. Not the enemy."

The words made Jim's face go hot for a moment; Maureen knew. She'd figured it out, but still loved him. Suddenly, holding her in the dark and hearing her sleepy voice made Phu Hoa Dong feel like a bad dream—not real at all. So after breakfast, Jim took Sue-Sue for a ride.

"A little tour," he told his daughter-in-law.

"Thanks, Dad," she said. Amy never called him "Dad" before. Made him blush.

In the golf cart, Sue-Sue bounced up and down. She giggled and squealed. Somewhere along the crisscross of paths, Jim discovered that he loved the music of her voice. *My granddaughter*, he thought, trying the word on as if it were a new coat.

"You look like sherbet," he said. She was wearing a smock that was the color of limes.

"You look like chocolate pie," she said.

"Chocolate pie?"

"With lots and lots of whipped cream."

She was being silly. Jim could see that, and he laughed.

"Want to see something special?" he said. Sue-Sue nodded and squealed, so Jim drove the cart down to the twelfth hole, to the felled tree that he and Maureen found last week.

"This is their home now," he explained. "They were displaced from their natural habitat." Sue-Sue looked confused. The word *habitat* was a little over her head. He rethought and said, "They had to find a new place to live, just like me and Grammy."

She understood. Smiled. "They go hiss?" she asked.

"They go hiss," he said.

Inside the rotted tree was a nest of coral snakes. They were twisting and turning around each other in knots of color, a kaleidoscope of red and yellow, true as jewels.

"Red and yellow, kills a fellow," Jim said. "Red and black, won't hurt Jack."

Until that moment, he'd forgotten he'd learned that in Phu Hoa Dong.

Sue-Sue laughed. "The babies are small like me," she said and held her arms out to Jim. Her face glistened with sweat. The doe eyes. It overwhelmed him.

He gave her a push.

For a moment it felt good; he felt relieved. Payback time. I'm not weak. I can't be fooled again, he thought.

Then Sue-Sue fell backward, and the snakes jumped.

That's about all Jim remembers clearly. That and the sound of her voice, a granddaughter's voice—not "Cong," "Charlie," or "Chuck." It was a granddaughter's voice— confused and afraid.

He remembers that—and the ambulance ride.

Maureen breaks through the surface of the water right next to him.

"Go away," she says.

"Sue-Sue's okay."

"I'm not."

"It was an accident."

Jim wants to believe that so much he nearly does.

Maureen starts to say something else, but stops and looks up. The Thunderbirds have regrouped. Jim looks at his watch. 12:41. Time for the finale. One by one, each airplane dives low, just above the tree line, then holds steady. They circle each other, closer and closer, until it looks as if they are linked in an impossibly tight circle.

Jim imagines the pilots leaning hard to the left, steering with their bodies, trying to keep the thin wire control steady, the circle tight. Man, that's tough, he thinks, and a single plane begins a nosedive into the center of the circle. Jim figures it's going top speed, about 1,145 MPH, straight down. There's no room for mistakes.

The water in the pool vibrates. Jim reaches across and touches Maureen's shoulder. She's startled. Jumps a bit.

"Forever," he signs.

Her face softens. Jim can see that she remembers their

wedding. She has that look on her face he knows so well. But then she shakes her head.

"Forever is too long a time," she signs back.

Her eyes are filling with tears again. Jim lets go of her arm. They stand together, yet apart, watching the planes. Not looking at each other. Awkward. They watch as the pilot pulls out of the dive and then disappears. One by one the other planes follow, faster than words.

Jim can hear his father's whistle, clear as day.

He imagines there are a father and his son waiting in the woods somewhere in America, lost in a seemingly endless fall day, with the smell of blood on their hands and the sound of a ghost whistle, low and dark.

In the spiky green grass, Jim can see the small green snake shed his skin against the stone edge of the pool cage. It then moves on, raw and reborn.

The jets break the sound barrier.

In the moment of eerie silence that follows, Jim says, "I'll miss you," but he's too late. Maureen can't hear him. The sound barrier has been broken.

The air around them is filled with thunder.

◆

Subtitled

IN THE MONTHS BEFORE HER MOTHER DIED, Sophie decided that she would speak only French to her. Her mother didn't speak French, and Sophie found that convenient.

"*Au revoir, Madame!*"

"Sophie, damn it to hell! Don't make me take a swipe at you."

Sophie's mother, Marietta, was only seventy-one years old when she died. She was pink, poodle haired. Dentures optional. Had a mean right hook.

Sophie, who was once a premed student, had analyzed her mother's swing with a near surgeon's eye. Not only did the older woman have an abnormally long humerus, but every finger on her right hand was adorned with a chapter from her marital history. This made her lethal.

On her distal phalanx was a quarter-carat princess cut diamond from her first husband, Jack. Sophie knows only three things about her mother and Jack:

Jack married Marietta when she was sixteen years old.

Jack was her English teacher.

Marietta had just written a book review on a new book, *Lolita*. Jack gave her an A.

That's more than Sophie feels she ever needs to know.

On her mother's middle phalanx was a waxy-colored emerald from her third husband. Sophie could never remember his name exactly. It was Don, or Dan, or something like that. Sophie's mother and that particular version of husband were married in 1973 for about two months.

On her mother's proximal phalanx was Sophie's favorite ring: a ruby that her father, Joe, Husband Two, gave Marietta when Sophie was born. It's small and round, like she was. It was perfect—at least to Sophie.

On her mother's thumb was an anniversary band of suspect-quality topaz from Alex, Husband Four and Five. Sophie never met him, but she had to admire his courage for going two rounds.

Finally, on Marietta's pinky was a gold butterfly, an engagement ring from a man who is only known to Sophie as "The One That Got Away." Lucky bastard.

So when Sophie's mother hit you with her right hook, it was a lot like being sideswiped by Gordon's Jewelers.

As Sophie used to say, "Love hurts."

Unlike her mother, Sophie never married, even though she was a striking woman. A little round for modern standards, but her hair was amazing. Always unruly, undisciplined: made her seem petulant. Sophie wore it long to her waist because someone once told her that she looked like a painting by Peter Paul Rubens. Butchers loved her. Dry cleaners gave her extra starch. There was always a cookie for her from the baker. The mailman weighed all her packages twice, just to be on the safe side.

Sophie's interest in the French language began shortly after she moved her mother from Ohio to Florida and bought her a trailer in a very nice park right down the street from her own apartment. In retrospect, it seemed inevitable. Sophie was not used to having a mother. Marietta was not used to being had. And, as soon as she unpacked, Marietta realized that her daughter was broke and—given her unusual skill sets, which included the ability to clean and filet blowfish—would always be broke.

So Sophie's mother did what she felt was a reasonable thing to do. The only thing she could do. The one thing any mother in her situation would do. Marietta began an unrelenting campaign to force Sophie to marry someone. Anyone.

"Marriage means money," Marietta said.

"I don't even have a boyfriend," Sophie whined.

"We're not talking boyfriends; boyfriends go dutch. We're talking husbands. How hard is it to find a husband? You go to a party. You lift up your skirt. You run a credit check. Next thing you know, I'm throwing rice at you."

"Shouldn't I run the credit check before I lift up my skirt?"

"Don't make me swipe you!"

"I'm young. I'm focusing on my career."

"You're thirty-six! You're nearly dead! Career? What career? You've been an exotic dancer, a minister, a massage therapist—"

"I am what is called a 'career careerist.'"

Even though Sophie had just made up the term, she believed it with conviction. There was an excitement in her voice, a lilt that careened one way, then the other.

"My career is the art of having a career. What I actually do doesn't matter. It's not the point. The doing is not important. I'm about process. The process of being in a career is the point.

"It's all very Buddhist," she said.

And Marietta swiped her.

After that, Marietta signed her daughter up for bridal registries at Pottery Barn, Target, Saks Fifth Avenue, and Burdines. Then Williams-Sonoma. And Kohl's. Then Stein Mart, K-Mart, and Home Depot.

Soon every store with a registry within a fifty-mile radius of Sophie's Sarasota home had a "Sophie Burnham" registered. The wedding date was always TBA, as was the name of the groom. When the stores started sending congratulation cards, Sophie called her mother.

"So this was not a joke?"

"You have to be ready!" Marietta said. "A Society for the Blind convention could come into town, and bingo! Oh, the disability pensions they have! Big money! Easy living!"

And so, this was not a joke.

Sophie had nothing against marriage. If she could meet a man like her father, she'd marry him in a minute. Joe was a circus acrobat with Rat Pack hair who worked as a gas station attendant but was always in training. Once, when a customer drove in, he cartwheeled all the way to the pumps.

Instead of "Fill 'er up?" he shouted, "Ta da!"

He was an amazing man. He could pull quarters from his nose. And he liked jokes, knew a lot of them.

"Knock, knock," he'd say when he came home at night.

"Don't make me swipe you!" Sophie's mother would reply.

To the best of Sophie's knowledge, her father was the only one of Marietta's husbands who left her a widow, although it was more by default than intention. He moved out while Sophie was at school one day, but never signed the divorce papers. He also never called, or wrote, or explained. He just vanished.

Sophie told all her friends that her dad left to join the circus. She was ten years old at the time. She imagined him on the high wire balanced on one leg, pulling quarters out of his nose, or teaching the lions to do cartwheels. Sometimes, she imagined him as the main event. He would be dressed in a silver leotard, handcuffed, locked in a box, and submerged in water. Disappeared.

"Ta da!" he'd shout, but no one could hear him.

So Sophie went to sleep every night knowing that her father was circus busy, too busy to call, but that he still loved her and thought about her all the time.

Then, one hot July night, Sophie saw him on the news. Actually, it was just a shoe by the side of the road. His truck overturned in a ditch.

"Ta da," Sophie whispered. The words crumbled.

Marietta said nothing, locked herself in the bedroom, and wouldn't come out for two days.

Sophie kept a picture of her father on her dresser: Joe, as proud father, at a backyard barbecue. In the photograph, he is tall and gawky like Sophie. Perpetually twenty-four years old and wearing a chef's hat rakishly tilted to one side. He looks like all young men who suddenly find themselves in the role of father do—overwhelmed, embarrassed, and naked in his love. Sophie is just an infant, squinty eyed and red as meat. She fits in the crook of his arm. In his free hand, there's a T-bone speared on a long fork. He seems to be trying to feed it to her. Sophie is about a month old. She's pretty sure she didn't have teeth yet, but appreciates the gesture. It says to her that her father wanted to give her the very best, right from the start.

He gave her T-bone love. That's how she thought of him, always. Her one and only T-bone love.

Her mother had a different take. "He was a nutcase. Crazy! Look: dripping bloody meat on a baby! What kind of father is that?"

Sometimes when Marietta said this, she spat on the ground as if to ward off his evil spirit. But sometimes, she sounded wistful.

T-bone love all the way: that's what Sophie had planned to give her mother, that's why she moved her to Florida. There was only one problem with her plan. She couldn't afford it. Sophie had to take a lien out against her house to buy her mother the trailer. But she did it anyway. She had to. Sophie was drowning in mothers.

In Sarasota, mothers were everywhere. There were mothers who sat at tiny French cafés and sipped white wine and talked about opera, mothers who let their sons push the cart as they shopped for artisan cheeses, mothers who wore black turtlenecks and their hair in silver crew cuts, and mothers who went to the film festival and flirted shamelessly with the ancient directors whom nobody quite remembered anymore. There were even mothers who painted, mothers who taught yoga, and mothers who ate only raw food. There were so many interesting mothers in Sarasota that Sophie wanted one of her own.

Unfortunately, what she got was Marietta.

"Damn it to hell, Sophie! Florida is filled with old people! I hate old people! They piss their pants and smell!"

Sophie and her mother had been out of touch for a long time. It wasn't planned. It just happened. One Sunday Sophie forgot to call. She was twenty years old and moving to Florida to become a Mennonite. So, on some level, it was understandable. Things were a little hectic. Sophie really knew nothing about the Mennonites except that they owned a lot of beachfront property, rode bikes, and made pies. It sounded like it might be a good career choice for her. So she moved to join them.

Pretty soon, Sophie discovered that being a Mennonite wasn't as easy as it looked. She had to learn restaurant management, because those pies had to be sold somehow, and marketing, too.

Soon, Sophie became part of an outreach team that put together a catalog sales division for jams and pretzels. They later added rocking chairs and gliders.

It was a heady time.

Eight months went by before Sophie finally remembered to call her mother. But it was too late. Marietta had married Alex and moved, and the number was disconnected.

Sophie lost her. She began to think she had a habit of losing parents.

A few months later, Sophie left the Mennonites to join

the Hare Krishna. Seemed like a strong lateral move. She liked airports and felt she looked good in saffron. No one in the Hare Krishna had a mother—or, at least, one they spoke to—so Sophie forgot all about hers. That's what she told herself, anyway.

Still, it did come as a surprise when, sixteen years later, she began to think of her mother again. Constantly. Dreamed of her. Of course, it really was inevitable. Sophie lived in a town filled with so many mothers that she had accidentally run over one who was jaywalking. Birdlike, the old woman flew off the hood of Sophie's car. Squawked. And so Sophie suddenly began to wonder where her own mother was. What she might be doing. If she still was afraid to fly.

The judge let Sophie off on probation but warned, "Somebody's mother is everywhere. You have to pay more attention."

So Sophie did. She Googled her own and found that Marietta was still living in Bryan, Ohio. Bryan is the birthplace of Dum Dum suckers, Etch A Sketch, and Sophie—although Sophie was then currently telling people she came from Sweden because she managed a Scandinavian furniture store.

So every Sunday, Sophie, the prodigal daughter, would call her mother long-distance. Marietta would tell her stories of how one neighbor shot another, or how she had to eat cat food because somebody broke in and stole her pension check, or how cold she was. "No heat! Damn it! This apartment has no heat!"

Marietta clearly needed saving. All the husbands were

gone, one way or another. Friends had faded away. It seemed to Sophie that she was all Marietta had left.

"Why don't you come to Florida?" she asked after a time. "I could find you a place. Something small. Put it in your name. A gift. Just for you."

"Florida?" her mother shouted. "There are roaches and sharks. Are you trying to kill me?"

Still, every conversation would end with her mother saying, "And nobody gives a damn. You'll see what I mean. You'll die old and alone and miserable, just like me."

So Sophie kept asking and finally, one Sunday, Marietta agreed. The next day Sophie took out a loan to buy a small white trailer on a large corner lot with orange and mango trees and a resident blue heron named Sam.

Sophie was suddenly filled with purpose. She'd never saved anybody before. She felt reborn. She decided to make a new start for herself, too. She changed her name from Sophie to Zen, and opened the Intuitive Counseling Center in a small beachfront office complex on Siesta Key. She avoided using the word *psychic*—it sounded so unprofessional—but did purchase a flashing neon hand because she'd always been a sucker for tradition.

The sign worked. Right from the start, Sophie/Zen was booked solid. Though not often right about the future, she had a mystic air about her engendered by the fact that she had, almost by accident, begun to tell people she was Native American.

"My tribe called me Deer-Seeker," she was fond of saying. "In the winters, I kept us from starving."

That always produced a nice tip.

Still, it was difficult for her to make enough money to live on and support her mother in the manner that other Sarasota mothers enjoyed. Beachfront rent for the Intuitive Counseling Center was high, and tourists often balked at paying full price for a session.

"Don't you have an early bird special?" they'd say. "It's Florida! Everybody has an early bird special!"

So every now and then she'd have a "bank liquidation sale." "Your future at rock-bottom prices!" the banner read.

A line of tourists would form about 6 AM.

Despite her busy schedule, Sophie, as Marietta still adamantly called her, always made time for her mother. She spoke to her every morning at 7 AM, and when she had a little extra money, she bought Marietta new clothes, or took her to charity events or wine tastings.

Marietta told everyone they were sisters. They once went to the piano bar at the Ritz, and Marietta sang "My Funny Valentine" to the tune of John Denver's "Country Roads." And even though security often escorted them out of events, her mother would sometimes seem pleased.

Every Saturday, Sophie and Marietta went to the farmers' market. It was Sophie's favorite thing to do. The market was downtown on Lemon Street. It was small but quaint. Smoke from her mother's cigarettes formed a thick cloud around them, and people stepped out of the way as Marietta would poke and bruise the perfect rows of white eggplant, sniff the head-on shrimp, and shake the clams—"guaranteed perfect," twenty-five for eight dollars—like dice. People stared. Talked. It was nearly like being a movie star.

On these mornings, Marietta did most of the talking. She had many pet phrases that she'd return to over and over again:

"Out of my way, fat ass!"

"How much? You crazy?"

"Everybody tries to screw you!"

And Sophie's favorite: "If another bitch pushes me, I'm going to have to swipe her."

On Saturday mornings, while they strolled through the farmers' market as other mothers and daughters did, Sophie/Zen was willing to forgive her mother everything— the lack of home-baked cookies, the nights she'd had to sleep on the front lawn when Marietta had "sleepovers" with men she'd met at the shopping mall. Even the time when Sophie was fourteen years old and her mother had tried to marry her off to the manager of McDonald's. "You'll be rich!" she told Sophie. "And think of all those french fries!"

On Saturdays, it was all forgiven. Having a mother was that much fun. For about six months.

Unfortunately, one Saturday, things changed.

Sophie was looking over some free-range eggs when she saw her mother take a perfect tangerine, slip it in her pocket, and walk away.

And the farmer saw it, too.

Sophie handed the man a dollar. "For my mom," she said. "Keep the change."

"Two dollars," he said. "Bad year for fruit."

So Sophie pulled the last bill from her wallet and handed it to him. The dollar was a little wet from the sweat of her hands.

The man smirked. Shook his head. "These old ladies," he said, "they think we owe them the whole frickin' world."

Sophie, ever the actress, smiled knowingly. "What can one do?" she said in a voice that was cashmere and credit cards. "They *so* depend on us."

"And on Depends," he said and laughed.

And Sophie laughed, too. Just to be polite, to not make a scene. She felt a little woozy. Sick to her stomach.

Unfortunately, none of this exchange escaped Marietta. She was red faced, puffing. "What the hell you do that for? You see those prices? He can afford it. You can't."

"I did it for you," Sophie said. "It's shoplifting. He could have had you arrested."

"You did it for yourself. To show off to that guy. To make me feel like a smelly old fool."

All around them, mothers and daughters were staring. Sophie felt her face color.

"I did it because I love you," she said quietly. Sophie hadn't told her mother that she loved her in such a long time that the words seemed to belong to another language, a language she had once learned and then forgotten.

"*Je t'aime,*" she said to clarify.

For a moment, Sophie thought she saw Marietta's face soften as if she had remembered Sophie as a baby, remembered that first moment she held her small pink body in her arms. Sophie leaned in, remembering it, too. She was so close that she could smell the soap on Marietta's skin. Ivory: 100 percent pure.

It floats, Sophie thought. Then remembered. *Floats away. Disappears.* On reflex, she reached out as if to catch her mother, to hold on to her.

Marietta jerked away. Threw the tangerine at Sophie, who ducked. "Love is bullshit," she said. "Everybody's got an angle."

There was an ache in her mother's voice. It stunned Sophie. "How is *love* an angle?" she asked. *Disappears,* she thought again.

"Go to hell," Marietta said. "I'm moving out of here. Going home."

Sophie wasn't quite sure she heard her mother right. "What do you mean? Isn't this your home now?"

"This is your home. I'm your charity case."

"You're my mother—"

"You don't even know what that word means. *Mother.*" Marietta didn't say the word so much as spit it.

The two women looked into each other's eyes. Sophie's heart beat: trapped, a hummingbird. Marietta grabbed Sophie by the arm. Leaned in close. Sophie could smell her mother's sour skin; she held her breath.

"Here's what I learned through seventy-one years of life and a shitload of marriages," Marietta said. "Everybody is in it for themselves. You. Me. Everybody. Love means shit; there's always an angle. People say they love you and leave. Always. That's what everyone does, and the person who tells you different is the first one who'll screw you—and that's my bit of motherly advice."

Then she let go of Sophie's arm and stood there, defiant. Her blue eyes murky, unreadable. "I am not your fool, or anyone else's. I'm going back to Ohio."

"Why?"

Marietta had no answer.

Sophie was rocking back and forth on her heels the way she used to when she was a little girl. Arms wrapped around her body.

You'll ruin the heel of your shoes, she could hear her mother say, but knew it was too late for that now, those days were long gone. Still, she wanted to hear it.

When Marietta finally spoke, *your sister* is what she said. "Your sister called. Just this morning. She wants me to live with her."

Sophie stopped rocking. "What sister?"

"You don't believe me?"

"I didn't say that." Sophie was stumbling for words. "It's just that, well, you never said anything before. It seems so unbelievable that you wouldn't say anything—"

"Well, I am now," Marietta said darkly. "Alex's girl. She just married a banker in Ohio. She has a huge house in Ottawa Hills now. And three children—he was married before—and they both drive a new Cadillac—"

"Why didn't you mention it before?"

"You never asked."

"Well, what's her name?"

Marietta hesitated, "Cheri."

Sophie felt her mother was lying, but Marietta continued. "Cheri has blue eyes like Alex did. Blue green with gold specks. She's very beautiful. And young. And now rich."

Sophie felt like she was being punched. "I don't understand."

"It's simple. She can afford me. You can't afford a piece of fruit."

The two women stood in silence and studied the lines in each other's faces. Committed them to memory.

Sophie was the first to speak. "Then why'd you come in the first place?" she said. *Love*, Sophie thought. *You came for love.*

For a moment, Marietta seemed to soften as if she heard what Sophie was thinking. Then shook it off.

"I've had enough of your crap," she mumbled, seemed unconvinced.

Sophie caught her mother's arm. "This is just a joke, right?" she said. *Please be a joke*, she thought.

"If I would have known that I could live like a queen in Ohio and not in some sardine box of a dump, you think I would have come here?"

"I don't understand."

"I can't explain it any clearer. Look, if I were you and you came to live in my town, I wouldn't give you a thing. Not one cent."

"That's not true."

"But it is. When you were my kid, I never gave you anything more than I had to. I never wanted to. I kept whatever I could for myself, for my own life. And now, all these years later, you keep giving me everything—clothes, lunches, fancy dinners—and I don't have any idea why."

Sophie could feel the truth in this, the shame. T-bone love, she wanted to say, but all she could say was, "I really don't understand."

"WHAT don't you understand? Don't you speak English?"

Sophie looked at her mother in the hot sun of the market, and she seemed to fade away before her eyes. Like a photograph. Like a photograph on Cheri's mantle.

"*Non, Madame,*" she said sadly. As they walked through the rest of the market to the car, Sophie only spoke French.

"What is this? Torture?" her mother finally said.

"*Oui, Madame,*" Sophie said and ducked. It was torture.

Sophie never saw her mother again. She called her once, but Marietta hung up, so Sophie didn't call back.

A few months later, there was a message on Sophie's answering machine. It was the manager from her mother's trailer court. "Sorry," he said. "She had me as the next of kin. I don't know why."

Sophie's mother was dead. In Sarasota, not Ohio. She had never left.

"Feisty broad. Had cancer real bad," the manager said. Then he showed Sophie the obit he'd written for Marietta. "It was the least I could do."

"She went out fighting," it read. Short and accurate. It said nothing about the multiple husbands. The mean right hook. Or Sophie. Or Cheri, who may or may not have existed. But it was exactly what Marietta would have wanted.

"She would have liked that," Sophie told the manager. "Thanks."

Then he told her that there were instructions left. The body was to be cremated. No services. No visitation by anyone—not even next of kin.

"Sure."

"Sorry."

Marietta had vanished.

Lost another one, Sophie thought. *Ta da.*

Sophie walked down to her mother's trailer. The sun was just setting; the sky was hazy. The trailer park felt deserted. Under the cool blue streetlight, the corner lot looked smaller than Sophie remembered. As did the trailer: neat and white. She could see the orange tree in blossom, its flowers like stars on its branches. The mangos, the color of sunset, hung ripe and low.

Someone had rolled Marietta's trash to the curb for pickup. Fat bees swarmed the can. Hummed. Sophie shooed them away and took off the lid, just to see. There was a black plastic bag filled with garbage and a few things tossed on top: some new crew socks, a stained T-shirt, three bottles of nutmeg, and a book.

The items were so personal; Sophie felt like a stranger. She looked around to see if anyone was watching. For a moment, she imagined she saw the curtain of the trailer pull back, her mother's face, sharp eyed and wary. Sophie flinched out of habit. Then picked the book out of the trash. It was new, the price tag still on it, but its spine had been broken. *Conversational French.*

It smelled of her mother, that odd mix of sweat and cigarettes. Sophie put it in her pocket.

"*Au revoir, Madame,*" Sophie said. Then corrected herself. "*Mamam.*"

◆

Deals

EDEN AND BOB never touched in public. She drove. He didn't. She was big. He wasn't. She had a walled eye. He had bad teeth. Her good eye always seemed to be searching for a deal—something dented, something beyond its expiration date, a little bulge. He wrote the checks.

It was the perfect setup.

We couldn't afford a car. Eden and Bob couldn't have kids. "It's a little deuce coupe," that's what Mother used to say. She learned English by listening to rock and roll, but I knew what she meant. In Florida, in the summer, buses were pressure cookers. A station wagon with faux wood panel sides was Top 40.

We met them in the summer of 1973. Mother was Paris personified: wraparound Ray-Bans, ice blonde hair, Pall Mall halo. She was a blue angel chain-smoking her way through my youth. My sister Maggs was three. She still had that baby smell and a roller-coaster laugh. Threw off sparks.

It doesn't matter how old I was. I was just too old, that's all. Pink with fat. Stub brown hair.

Every Saturday they'd come. Eden with her walled eye drove. Bob sat in the back. On his lap he had the quilted tote bag that held their two Chihuahuas: Pepe I and Pepe II.

They were champions in their own small world. Classified as "teacups," they were tiny yellowed cups. Chipped barks.

At 9 AM sharp, Eden and Bob and the Pepes would honk the horn once. Only once. Eden warned us that if we weren't ready, she'd leave. "I've got better things to do with my time."

We were always ready.

The grocery store was a cool dream, but Bob never came in. He'd just sit in the car and talk to the dogs. "Oh babies, I won't leave you in the big hot car all by yourselves! No way, Pepes! No way!"

As we walked across the parking lot, we could hear him say this over and over again. It was the only time I can remember the dogs silent, their secret eyes watching him, unblinking.

Inside, we all knew our roles. Mother steered the cart and added up the bill as we went. The beans, the small bit of cheese: she carefully arranged each item so nothing would break. Or bend. Or bruise. Eden carried Maggs and made cooing sounds. I just was.

Every now and then, Eden would slide something into the cart. Cab fare, she'd explain.

"You don't mind, do you?" she'd ask and toss in a leg of lamb or a porterhouse. "It's just like Monopoly money, right Gigi?" she'd say.

The food stamps were orange and blue. Colorful. I guess that's what she meant.

My mother never answered. She just recalculated our total in silence, readjusted her list accordingly.

She hated that name, Gigi. It reminded her of Maurice

Chevalier. He always seemed happy, no matter what. "He ain't nothing but a hound dog," she'd say whenever an old movie of his was on. She didn't turn the channel, though. She'd sing along, "Gigi, that funny little . . . something . . . something . . ."

It was difficult to make out the words. When she sang in French, her voice grew thick.

My mother's name was Gisele. It was her grandmother's name. Mother always told us that her grandmother was a lucky woman. "She was old; the Germans had no need for the elderly."

That's all she ever said about the war. The numbers tattooed on her arm said the rest.

We met Eden and Bob at the public pool. It was our fifth summer in America, four months after my father died.

The pool was a chlorine dream. Maggs and I, bobbers in the shallow end, spent the summer diving for pennies. A wild toss over the shoulder sent us scrambling. My mother's laughter: a waterfall breaking over us. Maggs was our koi, my mother said, our fish of luck.

Graceful in the curved blue of the pool. Bob circled her. Silent. We didn't notice until he snatched the penny from her hands.

"Mine, now!" he said. His eyes, overripe. Maggs didn't cry, just blinked. He picked her up, high over his head, a prize. My mother, her mouth open, trying to find the right words. English not French. Not song titles. Something a stranger could understand.

"Put the baby down, Bob." Eden appeared from the deep

end of the pool. Startled us. The water flowed over her. Looked like she belonged at SeaWorld.

"Would she jump for a fish?" I wondered, then felt bad. Wondered how many times somebody thought that about me.

"Bob likes babies," Eden said to my mother, her stray eye, gray as sleet, watching me. A storm crossed over my mother's face, heat lightning. Maybe she didn't understand or maybe she did. "Would you like a beer?" Eden asked, pulling herself out of the pool.

The rush of water flowed hard; I was caught in the undertow. Bob still held Maggs. "Tidal wave! Tidal wave!" he screamed, laughing at the casual havoc Eden left in her wake.

I was swallowing hard. Chlorine and air. Couldn't touch bottom. Coughing. Red faced. Feet scraping the rough concrete. My mother's hand caught me; her wedding band cut into my waterlogged fingers.

"Looks like a bottom-feeder," Bob laughed. "I'd throw it back."

"Suzette, behave," my mother scolded, pulling me to my feet. No koi. Carp. Gray with nicked scales. "Take care of your sister."

But Bob had already seen to that. He held Maggs in his chicken bone arms. "Aren't you a perfect baby?" Eden asked her softly, reaching to touch the peach of her cheek.

"No!" Maggs shouted. Kicked.

"Magdaline, be nice to the lady." Mother was frowning, looking for a cigarette.

"No!"

Maggs squirmed. Mother mumbled apologies. Introductions were made. Bob bowed graciously, kissed my mother's hand.

"Sit down now, Bob," Eden said. "Please."

"You're no fun," he frowned, pretending to pout, and then spread sunscreen, thick as Crisco, over his pink chest.

"Suzette, watch your sister," Mother said, and I was dismissed. I sat on the edge of the pool, feet dangling. The toe of my right foot bleeding, just a bit. No scar this time. Maggs swam wild, rudderless.

Eden and my mother talked poolside, beer poured discreetly into paper cups. Their words like sand, eddied back and forth. Swift currents. After a few drinks, Mother told the story. My father. His Aqua Velva smell. Eyes like blue velvet, bluer than velvet. The busy street and how dangerous it was. I was goofing off. Supposed to help. The bus swerved. Swept him from his feet. A concrete angel. She didn't say it, but it should have been me. He pushed me out of the way. Maggs ran from the house, a box of bandages in hand. I didn't go to the funeral. Wouldn't speak, not one word, for more than three months. Only ate rice.

"Just rice?" Eden said. "That's strange."

"She went crazy," my mother whispered, her English almost perfect.

The sun baked my skin red.

That night, Mother told us Eden and Bob would drive us to the store every Saturday.

"Why?" I asked.

"Because they want to," she said and then sang to Maggs, "We'll have fun, fun, fun 'til her daddy takes the T-Bird away." Danced in circles. The Peppermint Twist. The Hully Gully. I just watched. Maggs fell over, laughing.

The last time we ever saw them, things went bad right from the start. 9 AM sharp. "We're having lunch," Eden said. "At the house."

"It is not time for lunch," Mother said.

Eden held Maggs close and opened the car door. "You smell like mothballs," Maggs said, squirming.

Eden brushed the front of her pink housecoat, as if to rid herself of the smell. "If you're coming, get in," she said quietly.

"Come on, Gigi. We bought some wine!" Bob yipped. "We'll liquor you ladies up, won't we, Pepes?" The dogs chipped in unison. Squeak toys. Bob had dressed them up in little Hawaiian print shirts. On their heads, small sombreros.

"Yip! Yip!"

We'd never been to their house. Ever.

Humidity: 98 percent. No milk. No choice.

"We just ate breakfast," my mother said, lit a cigarette, and slid in the back next to Bob. Eden hated smoking but didn't say a word. My mother puffed hard as we passed the supermarket. "Could we not stop for milk, just a moment?" she asked and exhaled tight between her teeth. Eden didn't answer.

Bob winked. "It's lunchtime in Paris, isn't it?" He began to sing, "Lunchtime in Paris . . ." The Pepes looked away.

Eden turned up the radio until the car vibrated country western.

"Crazy, I'm crazy for feeling so lonely . . ."

I hated that song.

"It's Patsy Cline," Eden said to my mother.

Bob sang louder, "Lunchtime in . . ."

"I really like Patsy Cline," Eden shouted over him. The dogs snarled. Yipped. Nipped at his fingers. He kept singing.

"Those dogs don't like you, Bob," my mother said, mostly to me.

"Sure they do," he laughed. "Everybody likes me. I could sell ice to Eskimos." He smiled; his teeth looked bruised. Eden drove faster. Twenty minutes later, we pulled up the winding driveway of a squat house. Ocean view.

"Gigi," Bob said, "play your cards right, and this could be yours."

"It is too early for lunch," my mother said slowly. Maggs stuck her tongue out so far it touched her nose.

"Feisty!" Bob laughed and slung the load of Pepes over his shoulder. The bag swayed. The tiny balls on their sombreros bounced like popcorn.

Inside the house, the air was heavy with velvet. Leather couches swirled like vines. Oriental carpets. I asked Eden were the bathroom was. "The Pepes will show you," she smiled.

"I've seen this trick a hundred times," Bob said. "We'll be in the kitchen." He took my mother by the arm.

"You'll like this, Maggs," Eden said. She removed the Pepes' hats, gaudy nylon shirts. "There, that's better, isn't it,

Pepes?" The dogs licked her cheeks. She made cooing sounds. Kissed the tops of their heads.

I looked away.

"Where are the bathrooms, Pepes?" She asked and placed them gently on the ground, as if they were indeed made of china. The Pepes yipped into action. Tiny toes skittered across the wood floor. Maggs and I followed close. We turned the corner, sharp, but didn't go into the bathroom.

At the end of the hall, the door was open. It was some sort of a storage room filled with hundreds of dolls. Boxes and boxes, balanced like jigsaw pieces. They still had price tags. Reduced 50 percent! Clearance! All of them were damaged somehow. There were barbies with broken pink sunglasses. Baby dolls without arms. Missing. Dented. Maggs didn't care. A tornado of desire, she dove into the center of it all. Plastic wrap flew like farmyard fences. It happened so fast. The first box tumbled. Then another. Then they all came down.

I don't remember the sound of the crash. I ran into the kitchen; the room was filled with balloons, crepe paper streamers. A sign read, "Welcome Future Amway Distributors." Boxes of detergent, soap, and solvents fanned the table like a hand of cards.

"Amway is the answer to your mother's prayers," Bob said to me. He was pouring Mother a glass of wine.

"Where is your sister?" she asked but could see it in my face. She knocked over the glass. Ran down the hall. Bob and Eden followed. I just stood there.

After a while Eden came back. "A bump," she said. The

Pepes were riding in her pockets. I could see myself in the dimes of their eyes. "They're still cleaning up. A lot of them got broken. Who's going to pay for that? Your mother?" Eden laughed. Then she started humming that song again. Patsy Cline. "Crazy." She put the Pepes on the table. Two huddled pears. A still life.

I wanted to say I was sorry but couldn't. That song. "Crazy." What do they know? People get different sometimes; they're not crazy.

"Rice is quiet," I said. That's why I ate it after my father died. I wanted her to know that. "I like rice."

Eden smiled. Her walled eye looked at the kitchen door and then at me. She put the two dogs in my hands. I'd never touched them before. They were cold. They shook.

"They're scared," Eden whispered, "but they'll let you kiss them." She leaned into me. "Everybody needs to be kissed," she said. Waiting. The Pepes trembled, licked my fingers gently. I never noticed that their eyes were blue. I could feel Eden's breath against my cheek. She smelled like Irish Spring and mothballs. "Everybody needs to be kissed," she said again.

She tasted like Sweet'n Low. Two drops is all you need.

I'm not sorry about the next part. I ran. I put the dogs in my pockets and ran. I don't know where.

It was almost dark when my mother found me. Streetlights shone like fat stars. She was red faced, as if crying, dragging Maggs behind her, bruised as fruit. I told her the story. Eden. The kitchen. Irish Spring. Mothballs. I didn't know why I took the dogs.

"They look like rats," she said, hands on her hips.

"Finders keepers," Maggs said. Kissed the tops of their tiny brown heads. She was laughing like the Fourth of July.

"What are we going to do?" Mother asked me. She picked up the dogs, one in each hand, holding them away from her like old fish.

"Can't we keep them?" Maggs asked.

"The doggies are not ours, Bijou." The dogs were silent.

"But they have blue eyes," I said, as if to explain. I took a Pepe from her hand. "See?" I held it so close to my mother's face, she could have eaten it with one bite.

"Blue eyes," I said again, wanted to say more, wanted to say I was sorry, sorry for it all. Wanted to say I was lonely for the smell of Aqua Velva and the gentle blueness of eyes. I wanted to say all that, but I didn't want to make her cry.

"Their eyes are real blue, see?" is what I said.

But my mother knew what I meant. She took a deep breath. "Bluer than velvet," she said.

Don't cry, I thought. The moment hung between us. Everywhere around us, the world was blue. The blind blue of twilight. The blue brine of tropical air.

And then the dog licked her nose. My mother laughed, and he licked it again. She kissed the top of his head. Then kissed his brother's head.

"Can we keep them, please?" Maggs started to kick.

"Do you like the name Elvis?" she asked the dogs. "We'll call you Elvis I and II, okay?"

The dogs yipped in unison.

"Yippee!" Maggs joined in, clapping her hands. I howled for good measure, too old to yip.

On the long walk home, the moon shone above us like a silver teaspoon at a garage sale. Maggs and I, laughing, fed the former Pepes, now Elvis I and II, stale animal crackers from a crushed box found in the bottom of my mother's purse. My mother serenaded us. "You ain't nothin' but a hound dog," she sang, stopping every now and then to explain the difference between the Peppermint Twist, made famous by Chubby Checker, and the plain old twist.

And all around us the world had become bluer than velvet.

◆

Relative Victories

MASON LOVES AIRPORTS. It's a recent turn of events. She'd never thought much about them before. But now, suddenly, she loves everything about them: the soothing public announcement system, the whoosh of the shuttle, and the comforting thud of luggage as it slides down the baggage claim chute like a luge. She spends hours walking the well-worn carpet in her comfortable shoes and sensible travel suit, but never gets on a plane.

Unlike most who live in Florida, Mason has not had plastic surgery. She is not tan. She does not wear shorts. She never drinks margaritas; lime irritates her acid reflux. She thinks the chorus to that song is "*Pasted* away again in Margaritaville," and so she sings it loudly, and a little off-key, when it seems socially appropriate. Mason drinks rum and Coke, tall.

"Wards off scurvy," her husband Peter used to say. It was his favorite drink. On weekends, when they both had the time, which wasn't often, they would sit on the three-season porch with the space heater glowing and plan Peter's return to his "ancestral homeland" of Florida.

"It beckons," he often said. Wistful. Peter wasn't born in Florida. He just felt a spiritual kinship.

"It was founded by pirates. Ransacked by pirates. Run by pirates. And, according to the last census, it is still home to most of the pirates in America. I need to be with my people."

Peter was a stockbroker.

"It is the favored profession of all landlocked pirates," he'd say at parties, and then laugh his stockbroker's laugh: his "set-them-at-ease" laugh, his "lull-them" laugh.

Mason loved that laugh. "A pirate's life for me," she said on their wedding day, and agreed that, no matter what, a little beach cottage with deep-water access would eventually be theirs. They even took a blood oath on it. Peter pricked her finger with a safety pin.

"This is silly," Mason said.

"Of course it is."

Within three years, they spent through her inheritance, but Peter remained.

"Fooled you, didn't I?"

He did. And so they decided to have a child. They named him Tyler and trained him in fencing, not football. "It'll come in handy," Peter told her. "Piracy is a genetic trait."

Tyler also became a stockbroker.

The first week that Mason fell in love with airports, she stopped at the rum bar in Airside E, Casa Bacardi, to have a drink. When she and Peter flew out of TPA, she'd never noticed the bar. Of course now, without distractions, Mason notices a lot of things.

"Tall," she told the bartender. "Lots of ice. No lime. Acid reflux."

The drink arrived sweating profusely. Mason didn't want to touch it. She just watched the sweat bead down the side of it and stain the cardboard coaster.

The bartender finally turned back to her. "How is it?" he asked. He had those knowing bartender eyes, the smooth bartender voice, the need to please. He was the kind of bartender you could tell anything to, comfortable as a couch. "Way you like it?"

Mason smiled. "Great," she said softly. The glass continued to sweat.

"Great," the bartender said, and turned away to pour another drink. Mason placed a twenty-dollar bill on the bar and ran to board her flight. Then did not board.

Mason could have gotten on that flight, and all the others that she's booked and rebooked in the past year. She always has a ticket. Her small carry-on bag always holds a change of wrinkle-proof clothes, a flannel nightgown, and three pairs of underwear. But when her flight is called she never gets on the plane.

No one ever questions her. She has a determined stride. You'd never mistake her for wandering aimlessly; she doesn't look the type. She is a mass of contradictions. Too young to be retired, but is. If you were to pass her on the concourse, Mason would look like the kind of person who knows where she is going and why, but isn't.

The city Mason is endlessly not going to is Chicago. She was born there. She and Peter lived their entire married life there: twenty-eight years. Her only child, Tyler, still lives there with his wife. At least, Mason thinks so. The last time she saw him was at Peter's funeral. He wouldn't even look at her.

Yet Mason calls every Sunday. She gets a recording, but she still calls. At first, she tried to call his office, but he wouldn't take her calls. She left messages: "Tell him that I'm sorry." The receptionist would only take her number.

After a while, Mason decided to go to his house. His wife, Pam, stood behind the door and watched her through the peephole. Mason could smell her perfume.

"Don't be a shit," Mason said. But her daughter-in-law still did not open the door. Mason knocked and knocked until finally the police arrived and asked her to leave.

"I could hear her breathing," she told the police officer.

He shrugged. "Kids *are* shits," he said. "Have three of my own." Then he escorted her car out of the neighborhood.

Despite it all, Mason still calls. She can't help herself. Sometimes she calls on other days: Tuesdays, for example. At 1 AM. The recording is always the same. The woman's voice is bright. Lovely. Comforting. Not judgmental.

"It wasn't my fault," Mason sometimes says. And sometimes says it over and over again, until the line, eventually, goes dead.

If anyone were to ask Mason about Chicago, she could talk endlessly about lake-effect snow and the subzero temperatures that can turn metal brittle, make it snap in your hand. "But there's no better shopping in the world than on Michigan Avenue," she could sigh. Or "the Berghoff! How could they close? What sauerbraten they used to make! And that strudel!"

But no one ever asks. Although, if anyone ever did, Mason has prepared a few bits of Chicagoan small talk that she knows have universal appeal. "What are we going to do now that Marshall Field's has been sold to Macy's? How can I get used to saying, 'Let's look at the Christmas windows at Macy's?' It just doesn't seem right. And Frango Mints! Macy's Frango Mints? It's un-American."

Mason has problems with change. She knows that. She's always known that. She used to like to say that status quo suits her. She has owned her Saab station wagon since 1992, when she bought it new. She has worn her hair long since the late seventies. She has had only one job in her life, at the Factory. She stayed twenty years and still remembers the smell of that place, that odd mix of stale urine, industrial solvent, and baby powder.

The Factory is an experimental school for juvenile offenders, part of the Chicago public school system. "It's just like teaching mainstream," the principal told Mason during her interview, "except there's lots of gangbangers and some of them are hard core, and some of them lifers—and all of them are scam artists.

"Do you think you can deal with someone like that? Somebody who has elevated lying to an art?"

"I'm married to a stockbroker."

Mason was hired.

Now, after all these years, she can honestly say that there

are at least four thousand people on this planet who may be functionally illiterate, who may have killed, raped, or robbed someone, but who, thanks to her, can recite Carl Sandburg's poem "Chicago."

Mason learned that poem in high school and considers it a moral compass. To her, it says, "If you are strong, you can be the master of your own world. You don't need anyone." And those kids needed to know that, so Mason taught it to every single student who passed through her doors, even if they were only there for one day. She's not sure they'd all thank her. But, as one of the more promising ones said, "it's better than cleaning toilets."

Relative victories, that's what Mason used to tell herself. As a teacher, you live for relative victories.

But, after Peter's death, she was asked to retire. The union rep told her that the psych exam came back as "iffy."

"Iffy?"

"Three days is a long time to wait to call for help," he said.

"I have issues with change," she said.

She was sent home.

Home—she can't even say the word now, doesn't know why. Still, when people ask where her home is, she shrugs and says, "everywhere," but still thinks, "Chicago."

Hog Butcher for the world.

Not much has changed since Carl Sandburg sang its glories, she tells herself. What was the soul of the city then is still there.

Mason knows that in the decades that she lived in Chicago, change did happen. She is not oblivious to change.

For example, the mayor changed six times, although two were called Richard Daley, a father and son, both a little pirate-esque, which was always comforting to Mason.

But everything else about the city, the important things, stayed the same. Peter's White Sox are still called the White Sox. Pizza is always deep-dish thick. Hot dogs are always covered with celery salt and sport peppers, unless specifically requested otherwise. And the starched shirt men still work overtime, still buy rum and cokes, tall, in plastic cups at the train station for the commute home, and still, slowly, became strangers to their families.

Building, breaking, rebuilding.

Since Mason arrived in Florida last year, she's held seventeen one-way tickets to Chicago; it only costs fifty dollars each time for her to rebook. She especially loves the airport late at night, when all the sleepy Chicagoans just want to take their sunburned bodies home. There's something magical about it.

"Airport Kismet," Mason would sometimes say to the person next to her. "The romance of travel. Can't you just smell it in the air?"

They could not. Seeping jet fuel, fast-food hamburgers, bathroom disinfectant, cheap perfume, diapers in need of changing: these were the actual things that Mason's potential fellow travelers could smell. But when Mason spoke of Airport Kismet in that wispy voice, and smiled her pirate smile, it was difficult to argue with her.

However, at 12:45 AM on St. Patrick's Day, when the flight Mason is not taking to Chicago becomes, officially,

4.5 hours late, and the young woman sitting next to Mason says, "Airport Kiss what? What the hell are you talking about?" she decides to scratch Airport Kismet and the extended discussion of the concept off her list of acceptable small talk topics.

The young woman next to Mason is drunk. Her words slur. Her baby is sleeping on its stomach in one of those woven baskets, like the kind you take to a farmers' market. Soft sided. Soft mattress. It's the kind of bed they warn you about, the kind of bed that a child can easily suffocate in. The woman holds the basket on her lap, and the soft sides of it curve in around the child. The baby doesn't stir, which makes Mason nervous, so she decides to keep right on talking.

"How old is your baby?" she asks.

"Leave me alone."

The young woman puts a protective arm across the basket. That's when Mason looks at her closely—the coal dark hair, the etched face. The girl looks like a student Mason once taught, a member of the Latin Queens who went by the name of Kahlo. She was unforgettable for many reasons, most of all her name. Gangbangers don't usually take the names of artists.

Mason's Kahlo was thirteen years old when she shot her best friend. Afterward, she tried to put the pieces of the girl's skull back together and then arranged her body as if she were just sleeping.

There was something about that act that affected Mason. It was both brutal and gentle at the same time. "Why take the name *Kahlo?*" Mason once asked.

"She was a true queen," the girl said. "At the funeral home when they tried to burn her body, she sat up—smiling—even though she was dead. They say her hair blazed like a halo.

"She was dead and on fire and smiling—like me."

Mason never forgot that.

And now, all these years later, the more Mason stares, the more this young woman looks like Kahlo, at least the way she would look seven years later. So Mason leans over and says, "You're Kahlo, aren't you?"

The young woman's eyes narrow. For a moment, Mason thinks that she sees a glimmer of recognition, but the girl says, "I said leave me alone. What are you, some kind of a crazy bitch?"

"Iffy," Mason corrects. "My therapist says I'm iffy—there's a difference."

And so, the young woman picks up her baby and rolls her suitcase across the room.

Mason is now convinced that it's Kahlo. She can tell by the way she walks: regal and defiant. Mason wants to ask her if she remembers the smell of the Factory, that odd mix of stale urine, industrial solvent, and baby powder—and if she remembers her. For some reason, Mason suddenly needs that girl to remember her.

She watches as Kahlo makes her way through the rows of bored and sleepy travelers: past the fighting young couple; past the preschoolers eating cold french fries from a Burger King bag; past the one-legged solider sleeping in the wheelchair with his rows of shiny new medals.

Once on the other side of the room, Kahlo puts her bags

down but does not check on the baby. She turns her back to Mason to make a phone call on her cell. The people around her read their magazines, watch the Weather Channel, and sleep. No one looks at the mother and child—it is as if she doesn't even exist.

Ghosts, Mason thinks.

Mason takes another Zoloft with the last of her warm Coke. A few minutes pass. The announcement finally comes over the loudspeaker: "Flight 456 is now ready for boarding. Passengers in Zone A, Priority Club members, people who need help boarding, and parents with small children please begin the boarding process."

Kahlo is distracted, crying into her phone. People are lining up to board. *Kahlo could miss the plane*, Mason thinks. Knows how hard it is to manage a baby and luggage in a crowd. *Screw "iffy."*

She goes over to the young woman, takes the cell phone out of her hand, slaps it shut, and says, "You'll miss the plane."

"You bitch—"

"Pirate," Mason says. "I prefer the term *pirate*."

Mason looks at the baby in the basket and has a sudden urge to hold him. *Just a minute, that's all. Tyler was so perfect at this age*, she thinks.

Overhead a voice says, "Will those holding tickets please board at this time?"

Suddenly, all around them, passengers push, curse, and swarm. They close up around the young woman, her baby, her bags. She is sucked into them. They push Mason forward.

Mason, the woman, her baby, the crowd: they are all moving as one—uncaring, unseeing.

"This is the last call. Those boarding flight 456—"

Mason looks around, and the young woman and her child are gone.

"Ticket?" a tired yet smiling agent says. Her braided red hair looks frayed, like rope.

Mason suddenly realizes that she is standing at the front of the line. There are dozens frowning behind her.

"Ticket?"

Not thinking, Mason digs into her purse and hands it to the woman. The agent tears off the stub. "Thank you," she says.

Suddenly, Mason realizes what she's done. The ticket is ruined. She can't use it again. An exquisite thin pain shoots across the left side of her face. Blurs her vision.

"Have a nice flight," the agent says, her voice strained.

Mason nods, and it feels as if bits of her scatter across the floor. The crowd pushes her forward again and onto the jetway. Once inside the plane, in her seat, buckled in, she thinks she sees Kahlo, two rows behind her. The attendant is helping a squirming baby into a car seat.

Where did the car seat come from? Mason wonders if the moment really happened at all. The pills make her feel so slow all the time. She takes out her cell phone and calls Tyler. The recording picks up again, as always.

"The number you have dialed is no longer in service."

The airplane engines whine. Mason listens to the message play over and over until the flight attendant taps her on the shoulder. "All cell phones must be turned off. We're trying to take off," he says.

"Sorry."

The flight attendant, a young man, is blonde and too tan—about Tyler's age. He looks at Mason closely. She can feel him size her up, imagines he notices that her pupils are dilated.

"Would you like me to sit with you?" he asks gently.

"I'm fine," she says, but doesn't sound fine. Her voice shakes.

"I'll steal you a fizzy water from first class when we reach cruising altitude," he says. "Nothing like an ill-gotten gain to perk a spirit right up."

As the plane speeds down the runway under the thinnest edge of a moon, Mason pulls her seatbelt tight. When they're airborne and level again, the attendant unbuckles. "Save this spot for me," he says and winks. Goes to get the drink cart.

Mason takes another pill. No water, she swallows hard.

Soon she is asleep and dreaming that she's free-falling through the sky. No parachute. A woman's voice says, "Wake up," and Mason opens her eyes to see Kahlo leaning over her. Or thinks she does; the drugs make her feel muddy, make the moment feel like it's part of her dream.

"Kahlo died long ago," the young woman says. "Everybody's got to bury their dead."

The dim cabin lights make the young woman seem luminous to Mason. She closes her eyes for a moment, trying to adjust to the light. Then Kahlo is gone.

Mason falls back into sleep, a dark dreamless sleep, until the airplane's thrusters shift into reverse and she wakes with a start thinking of Kahlo, the artist, smiling, her cremation fire ringing her head like a halo. *Bury your dead.*

The lights of Chicago can now be seen out the window, like so many small fires. Even in the darkness, the landmarks are still clear. The Sears Tower. Michigan Avenue.

"Final approach," the flight attendant says and sits down next to her in the empty seat. Mason fixes her hair quickly with her fingers.

"I stole you a water, but didn't want to wake you earlier," he says and hands her an elegant bottle—beautifully designed and clearly Italian. "Stuff it in your purse," he says. "Nobody cares. I palm these all the time."

The bottle is still cold. "Thanks." Mason puts it in her purse. She looks out the cabin window at the city. Her heart beats too fast.

"Beautiful, isn't it?" he says. "My hometown."

"City of the big shoulders."

"Sandburg, right?"

She nods.

"He got it right, didn't he?" he says. "And that part about laughing? Proud to be alive and cunning." He pauses. "What's the rest?"

"And strong."

"That's it," he says, and the plane bumps to a landing.

"Strong. That's the city . . . and that's the people, too. Isn't it?" He gives her that winning airline smile. Just like Tyler would have. Then moves quickly back into the aisle. Back to work.

"Home," Mason says as if trying on the word. Then she remembers what Peter always used to say: "Home is the place you build inside of each other's hearts."

Home, she thinks and unbuckles her seatbelt, gathers her bags, and walks down the jetway into the city of her birth. *Home.*

◆

Our Florida Vacation

THE MOTOR COURT IS AS PINK as it can be. Bill knows this place, told Luanne about it. Rainbow Village. He stayed here when he was a kid. That was a long time ago. Twenty-five years, at least, he thinks. It was nice back then. The sign hangs on a rusted hook: "Modern Efficiencies." Air conditioners are wedged into windows at odd angles. Dribble and wheeze.

The cottage Luanne is staying in is named Dopey. Doc and Sneezy are nearby. It reeks of bleach and mildew and the heavy heat of salt air.

"This is not your vacation," Luanne says.

"I know that," Bill says.

Bill and his mother stayed in Grumpy. He was nine. It was their little vacation. That's what his mother said. Bill's father wasn't invited. The bruise on his mother's face took nearly a month to heal. Bill never saw his father again.

Luanne has set Dopey's air conditioner on "Hi." Nothing happens. It's more like a greeting than a temperature setting. Frost wraps around its coils. Bill is profusely sweating in his orange jumpsuit. It's rolled up several times at the arms and legs. From a distance he looks like a prisoner, but he's a truck driver. He doesn't care. He likes his comfort.

Bill's a small man, unusually so. He has hands like soft dough, rolled and ready for the fryer. When it came time for college, his high school counselor Mrs. Robinson said, "The world has special plans for you," and handed him a brochure for the Ringling Bros. and Barnum & Bailey Clown College in Sarasota.

"You have to go with what God gives you," Mrs. Robinson said. Her teeth were small and pale as new corn.

"Thanks. I'll do that," Bill said, shook her hand, and then cashed in his college fund for the down payment on an eighteen-wheeler, fitted with the brake and accelerator on the dash.

"You got to go with what God gives you," he told his mother.

All these years later, Bill's truck still looks pretty good, a little worn but immaculate. It's candy apple red with a curtained sleeping area right behind the front seat. Old school. Airbrushed on the back is the phrase, "Running on faith and still 1,000 miles from nowhere."

The salesman suggested it. "Popular wisdom," he said, "gives a rig personality."

The words are faded now, but it doesn't matter. Bill still knows what it says, still remembers just how red candy apples can be.

Right now, in the parking lot, the rig partially blocks the driveway, but it doesn't seem to matter. It's the only vehicle out there, even though it's January, tourist season.

He looks out the window and shakes his head. It's difficult for him to see how this place has gone downhill. The month he and his mother spent at Rainbow Village was, and still sometimes feels like, the best weeks of his life. He fondly remembers the shuffleboard court: all the kids played there at night, betting nickels and drinking Yoo-hoo until their tongues turned chocolate black. Now the court is choked with weeds. Jesus, he thinks, I never wanted to see that.

Why'd Luanne come here?

Bill watches as she cracks ice out of metal trays into a blender, remembers his mother doing the same thing. But unlike his mother, Luanne stretches out like a highway. She's taller than Bill by nearly a foot. Her blonde hair is piled on her head like a worn bath towel. High-heeled sandals sparkle with cherry Jell-O jewels. She's wearing her one-piece bathing suit, metallic gold. It's standard issue for the underwater mermaids of Weeki Wachee.

Bill suspects she stole it, right before she quit.

"Don't get too comfortable," Luanne says. "You're not staying."

"Got a call from your landlord."

"He is so predictable." Her southern accent swoops and spins like a circus daredevil. Effortless, without a net. "Told you I went crazy, right?"

Bill nods. "Can you blame him?"

"No." She hesitates. "Bill, you need a girl who can love you back."

"Maybe I think that's you."

"You need a reality check."

"Is that why we're here?"

She shrugs.

"Listen, you left my childhood as your forwarding address, Luanne. I think I deserve an explanation."

She shrugs again.

Bill's eye is starting to twitch. He's never lost his temper with her, or anyone, but he's driven two days and a night to get here, and he's not in the mood. He counts slowly to ten. In his hand, there's a paper coffee cup from the I-75 Mega Stop in Valdosta. He grips it like a security blanket. The coffee is cold, of course. It's his gift to her. "Everybody needs a home, like on those Maxwell House commercials," she told him the first time they met.

Luanne was living in a battered women's shelter back then. Plastic surgeons laced her face back together the best they could, but even with a heavy layer of makeup you can still see her scars, like tiny train tracks, crossing and recrossing, destinationless.

When Bill first met her, she told him *Luanne* was her new name. With an outstretched hand, she showed him her new tattoo—a broken heart with the words "no more" written across the palm. "Every now and then I need to remind myself that you can't let your heart run wild."

Outside the motor court, traffic honks and shudders its way down Gulf Boulevard, but nobody turns in. Luanne carefully flips the pop-top of a can of Coco Loco with a butter knife. She's careful with her nails. They're pink as candied almonds. Real, not plastic.

Bill watches as she pours the coconut milk into the blender so gracefully it curves like a neck.

Beauty queen smooth, he thinks. Luanne once told him

that mermaids at Weeki Wachee are taught how to move with their heads and let the rest of the body follow, like the tail of a kite.

"That's the mermaid's secret," she said. "If you're not beauty queen smooth, you look like a worm on a hook."

Sometimes at night, they sit on the steps of his house, a tiny two bedroom painted the color of a peach left too long on the branch. Bill's head on her lap, she tells him the legends of mermaids. For example, how in Ireland they're called "Selkies" and could be either a seal or a woman—though not both at the same time.

"They're addicted to love, you know," she said. "They sneak onshore, shed their seal skins, take on as many lovers as they can. When they're done with 'em, they drown 'em."

"I'll make a note of that," Bill laughed.

When they were together, he laughed all the time. And so did she. He liked to hear her voice, the calliope of its music. Liked to watch her hair trail down her back like moonlight. He could listen to her for hours. And did. But now he wants answers. Things have gotten out of hand.

"How long are we going to be here, Luanne?"

Luanne turns on the blender, a rickety tornado.

Damn it, he thinks, but won't say it. His mother taught him never to swear and never to show his temper.

"The seeds of anger grow the Devil's fruit," she liked to say. Made him wonder what his father was like.

Still, he'd like to toss that blender across the room. The heat of the cabin is wearing on him. All he wants to do is to leave this place, forget he ever saw it again, curl into himself like a snail and sleep in the back of his truck.

Bill shouts over chewing ice. "Your landlord called me, that's how worried he was."

She turns the blender off. Bill's ears ring. "He wanted money, right?"

"What did you expect?"

"It's what I *don't* expect that I worry about."

Luanne presses the "crush" button. The blender kicks into high speed, screaming. She tosses canned pineapple into its glass jar. Pours in a jigger of blue curaçao. The drink turns the color of Tidy Bowl. The sight of it makes Bill queasy.

"Done," she says. Turns off the blender, and the Coco Loco tornado stops. She sniffs. Takes a sip. Frowns.

"Too much coconut. It's ruined."

"That's okay," Bill says, holding out his gift to her, a ragged paper cup. The seams bulge. "Want some?"

"Is it Maxwell House?"

He nods. The Maxwell House logo is printed on the cup. "Good to the last drop," he says and hops off the couch.

Bill removes the plastic lid for her so she won't break a nail. Luanne takes the coffee from his hand like a mechanical arm on the midway, reaching for a watch.

"Thanks," she says. Sniffs it. "That's nice, real coffee aroma."

"It's a little cold," Bill says.

"It's great." She takes a sip. "Good to the last drop."

She drinks it greedily. Her two perfect hands clutch the cup.

Bill wants to be that cup, but he doesn't move toward her.

Can't. He never makes the first move. She's out of his league. He knows that. Doesn't want to wreck it. Doesn't want to push.

Bill sits back down on the couch, feet slightly dangling. He feels like a child again, waiting to be told what to do. Waiting to be held. Just waiting.

He's very good at waiting. Considers it one of his best attributes.

Bill and Luanne met two years ago on Christmas Day. His mother had died the day before. Heart attack. He watched the paramedics work furiously as the revolving light turned the silver tree from red to blue to green. His mother loved that tree.

After they took her body away, Bill lay on her bed, unable to think of anything to do. After the holidays, there were papers to sign and arrangements to be made. Today, however, was Christmas Eve for everyone except the dead.

His mother's bed was scratchy pink. It smelled of her, spray starch and lilacs. Bill closed his eyes and fell into that odd zone on the edge of sleep. A chorus from a song raced though his head: "I know something about love." It was just the chorus, over and over again, all night long.

The next morning, Christmas, Bill packed away all of his mother's things.

It had to be done, he knew that, but he felt like a thief in a movie where the sound's not synchronized. His hands moved, but his brain felt a half a step behind.

Still, Bill was very tidy about the task. He washed, ironed, and folded all of her clothes. Packed them neatly in her suitcases. He cleaned her hairbrushes with Ivory Liquid, just the way she used to. Wiped away the dried pink rings of lotion from the lid of her Oil of Olay. He rolled her jewelry in her scarves so that the necklaces wouldn't tangle. He packed her things exactly the way she would have. The act felt as sacred as prayer.

When Bill was finished, he placed the suitcases in the attic. He and his mother had never stored anything up there. It wasn't air-conditioned. In the summer the temperature would rise to well over 120 degrees. Still, it seemed to be a good place for the suitcases.

Quiet, Bill thought. *Undisturbed.*

The suitcases were a red hard-sided Samsonite set his mother bought to come to Florida all those many years ago and never used again. Bill lined them up according to size. The 29-inch, then the 26-inch, then the round 24-inch that she used for her Sunday hats, and finally the squat makeup bag.

When Bill was finished, he stepped back to admire his work and noticed a brochure lying in the pink fiberglass.

"Visit Weeki Wachee! The World's Only Underwater Artesian Spring!"

His mother was always collecting brochures for him. "For ideas," she said. Places to take women he might meet on the road. On the cover of this one, a pleasant family peered into the clear spring: young boy, mom, dad. Inside, there were pictures of the famed mermaids: beautiful women wearing iridescent fish tails, drinking Coca-Cola underwater.

"Open 365 days a year. Even Christmas."

How this brochure made its way to the empty attic was a mystery to Bill, but he took it as a sign.

Despite the fact that it was Christmas Day, Weeki Wachee was packed. Most of the crowd were men alone or men with their kids, grinding their teeth. No noticeable wives, or women at all for that matter. Bill imagined their holiday meal, a turkey TV dinner with small cubed carrots. Just like his. Made him feel a little less alone.

The amphitheater was several stories underwater. The concrete steps seemed to go straight down. Bill held the center rail, not wanting to get pushed over, not wanting to slip. Despite the unseasonable heat, he wore his best suit, the one his mother had hung in the back of his closet, wrapped in tissue paper.

It was lightweight wool with pleats sewn in, double stitched for "rugged wear."

Bill and his mother bought it at the boys department at Sears. "Nobody will know where you got it," the saleswoman said.

Rugged wear—even the words made him sweat.

The amphitheater smelled of wet concrete. Looked a lot like Bill's high school auditorium. There were rows and rows of seats. Instead of facing a stage, they faced a huge plate-glass wall. Behind it was Weeki Wachee Spring, the entire spring held back by a single sheet of glass.

Maybe this isn't such a good idea, Bill thought, but it was too late to leave. He was sitting in the last available seat, front row center. The glass was just a few feet from his face.

The auditorium darkened. Over the loudspeaker a tinny voice supplied the details. "The spring presses up against the glass wall with the force of several thousand gs," it said. At least, that's what Bill thought it said. All Bill could focus on was the idea of the statement. *Any moment the glass could crack.*

"Enjoy the show."

Lights out.

The auditorium took on a bluish tint. Bill looked at his hands. They were blue, too. He turned around. All the faces of the men and their children were blue. It was like sitting at the bottom of a pool. Waiting. For a moment Bill felt afraid to breathe, felt he could drown.

Then, one by one the mermaids slid into the spring in a rush of bubbles, their long hair straight on end. They were waving. Out of reflex, Bill waved back.

The show was *The Little Mermaid* by Hans Christian Andersen.

"Some mermaids lure sailors to their deaths," the announcer said. "But the Little Mermaid gave her life for a love she could never have. She gave her immortal mermaid soul for love."

"Nice story," he thought, but these mermaids seemed very mortal, more mortal than most. They were tethered to breathing hoses and drinking bottles of Coke through a straw. They smiled and waved like den mothers. Bill was pretty sure that these were not the mysterious creatures Andersen envisioned.

Then she slid into the spring: the Little Mermaid.

Bill couldn't take his eyes off of her. She swam more gracefully than the others. Never seemed to need air. Never seemed to exhale. She looked as if she were made of liquid sapphire.

So blue, he thought, like love.

I know something about love.

The chorus of that song again filled his head. This time it made him giddy.

After the show, Bill waited for her by the employee parking lot. "Are you going to ask me what's the best tuna?" she said when she saw him. "I get that one a lot."

Bill shook his head. He hadn't planned to ask her anything. Or say anything at all. He only wanted to see her again, on dry land. The parking lot was nearly empty. The sun was setting; the sky wilted around it like a picked hibiscus. Bill suddenly felt ridiculous. He couldn't think of anything to say. So he held his program to his head, like a salute, and said, "Thanks a lot." Turned to leave.

His response was unexpected. It seemed to puzzle her. "Hey, I didn't make you sore, did I?" she said. "I was just kidding about the tuna thing."

"I'm fine," Bill said. Kept walking.

"It sounded kind of bitchy, though, didn't it? I didn't mean to be bitchy."

"It's fine," he said, but didn't turn around. He didn't want to make matters worse. He hadn't planned to say anything at all, and now it's clear to Bill that he's upset her.

Damn, he thought. I'm such an idiot.

He started walking a little faster.

"You know, it's Christmas," she shouted after him. "Want to get a cup of coffee? I know a place that sells Maxwell House."

Bill stopped.

The coffee shop was down the road, not far. They walked in silence in the damp evening air. The khaki lace of moss hung low on the trees, rustled like a skirt against ankles. Every now and then Luanne's hand would brush against him. Her skin was lotion soft.

They sat at the counter. Luanne rambled on. The spoon in her cup clicked, a castanet.

"You know," she said, "sometimes people ask me about the name, Weeki Wachee. What does it mean in Indian? Did the Indians have underwater mermaids, too? I tell them they did, only the air hoses weren't made of plastic because it hadn't been invented yet, and they never had underwater ballet, because of the same reason."

In the yellow light of the café, Bill could see the tiny white tracks that ran across her face.

"Are you lonely?" he asked.

Luanne didn't answer. Didn't look at him. He felt the air go flat. She ran her finger slowly along the chipped mug, its ragged edge. He looked around the coffee shop. They were the only customers. Silver cardboard letters wished him Merry Christmas. The waitress sat in the back booth smoking a cigarette, reading the holiday edition of the *Star*.

Time to pay the check, he thought, and raised his hand to get the woman's attention. Luanne caught it in hers. Held it for a moment.

"Why did you ask if I'm lonely?"

"It's Christmas. You're having coffee with me."

"A short guy?"

The words made his face go red. Bill nodded. "That'd be one way to put it."

"You think I feel sorry for you?"

"Short guys think that a lot."

She leaned over and kissed him softly on the lips.

"Would it matter if it were true?"

"No."

That night, Bill took her to his tiny peach of a house, the house that he and his mother had lived in all those years. He opened the windows. The smell of lilacs and spray starch was barely noticeable.

In the morning, Luanne made him a cup of coffee. Not Maxwell House, but it didn't matter to Bill.

"You know," Luanne said, leaning into him, "if somebody walked in right now, it'd be just like in the commercials. Good to the last drop."

Her skin smelled like summer to him. All heat and salt.

"Will you marry me?" he said.

She suddenly seemed sad. "Can't," she said. "I'm a mermaid."

Now, nearly two years later, her landlord called Bill. "You signed for her. You owe me," he said.

Luanne had painted everything in her entire apartment blue. The walls. The windows. The television.

"Even the damn toilet," the landlord said.

Bill just wants to know why.

The air conditioner cycles into a flatline hum. Bill walks over to it, puts his hands in front of it. No air. Nothing. Frozen. He turns it off. "We better open the windows," he says. "It's overloaded." He tries the window, but the crank is stuck. Rusted in place.

"Damn it," he says. "What are we doing here, Luanne?"

Luanne puts down the paper coffee cup. Holds her tattooed palm out to him.

"He found me," she says.

Bill reads the tattoo to himself over and over again, trying to adjust to the idea of Him. Adjust to Him coming back into her life. And into his.

Bill doesn't know His name, only knows that He was a jealous man, and that's all Bill needs to know. "So, what happens next?"

"Do you want to take a swim?"

"Shouldn't we talk about this?"

"I'd like to swim."

"I didn't bring trunks."

"You keep them in your truck, just in case."

It's true. Bill feels his face go red.

"Don't start lying to me now," Luanne says. "It wasn't so bad, you know, the apartment. I don't know what the landlord told you, but you should've seen it. Real soothing. I put an air conditioner in every room. One or the other is always kicking into different cycles. The harmony of cool makes the place sing a kind of a blue song, you know?"

A Miles Davis kind of blue, he thinks.

"What happens next?" he says again. He doesn't know what else to say. A blue apartment. The blue song. Tidy Bowl cocktails. And Him. He's back. How did He find her? If He found her, why isn't He here?

Logic suddenly feels like a Scrabble game with too many tiles missing.

"So, let's go swimming," Luanne says and kicks off her sandals. She opens the door of the small cottage. The heat is like a fist. "I'll meet you."

It appears that Bill has no choice.

Inside the truck, it's like an oven. Behind the front seat of the cab, his tiny sleeping compartment is neat, not like some others he's seen. Over the thin mattress he's taped a picture of his mother and a program photo of Luanne as the Little Mermaid. They look down on him with Siamese smiles.

The space is large enough for Bill to dress in. He jiggles out of his jumpsuit. Puts on his red swim trunks. They're new and stiff, never been worn.

Bill has a farmer's tan: arms only. His belly is like a snow-ball. He puts on a pair of plastic thongs and stands on the mattress and looks at himself in the rearview mirror. His head hits the ceiling. All he can see is a strip of Wonder Bread flesh. He shudders.

It's what's inside that matters, he tells himself, but takes a white dress shirt from his suitcase, puts it on. It covers his body but, without cuff links, the sleeves reach well past his fingers.

Outside the cab, heat rises from the asphalt in waves. Bill locks the truck, shoves his keys in the nylon pocket of his trunks, and walks across the unpaved parking lot. Burrs, crosshatched in the sand, stick into his pink feet. The closer he gets to the beach, the more his eyes water. Behind the pink rows of Rainbow Village cottages, the beach is a mess. Dead fish are scattered everywhere. A shark lies on its belly, next to a rotting stingray. A handful of catfish hums with the buzz of flies.

Red tide, he thinks. *Great.*

Bill hates the water in general. All he needs is the addition of a killer toxin to make his eyes twitch. He'd like to suck it up and just jump in, but it's difficult.

"You never know what's in there," his mother always used to say. "Horseshoe crabs with their razor tails will slice you up. Jellyfish will bump into you and stop your heart."

She could go on like this for hours; aquatic dangers were one of her favorite topics. So Bill hates all of it. Sharks. Rays. Red tide makes it worse, stuffs dying down your throat.

Still, in the distance, Bill can see Luanne. He has to go. No choice. She's far from shore, bobbing up and down on a raft. Fish are floating belly up in her wake.

She waves. He coughs.

"Red tide," he shouts, pointing to all the dead fish.

"I've got a raft," she says. Waves him in.

No choice at all. Bill takes off his white shirt and folds it carefully. Buttons the top button. He keeps his plastic flip-flops on. Waffle thin, they won't provide much protection if he steps on the stiletto gill of a catfish, or something worse, but at least they make him feel better.

"Come on!" Luanne calls. The gold of her suit flashes in the sun.

A wave breaks over his feet. A dead sea turtle washes in. Belly up and huge. Covered with barnacles.

Get this over with, Bill thinks, holds his breath, and runs into the water—flip-flops and all. Once past the shoreline, the undercurrent of the Gulf Stream rips the limp plastic away from his feet.

Shit.

His eyes are watering from the stench. His plump belly itches and is welting. Red splotches like continents form, make it look like the globe. Bill breaks into a butterfly stroke, churning the water as much as possible.

When he reaches the raft, he can see through his tears that Luanne is smiling. "The water's warm, isn't it?" she says.

He hadn't noticed. Now that he does, he thinks he has to pee.

"The water is your friend," Luanne once told him.

Can you pee on a friend? he wonders.

Luanne tosses a plastic towrope over the raft. The rope is bright yellow and thick, the kind they use on boats. "Tie it around your waist. It's safer."

The waves are high. Slap him in the face. Bill finds it difficult to keep above them, difficult not to breathe in water.

"It's a lifeline," she says, as if that explains everything.

Bill isn't sure if that's true or not, but with the unforgiving sun, the rotting flesh, and the red tide burning his skin like acid, he thinks the statement makes sense.

He takes the rope and ties it around his waist.

"There," Luanne says, "that's better now, isn't it?"

The raft she is leaning across is large, large enough for two, but Bill isn't sure how to board it without unbalancing them both.

"We're kind of far out, aren't we?" he says.

"Don't worry." Luanne kicks her feet. Pushes them out a bit farther. "I'm a mermaid, remember?"

Bill looks back at Rainbow Village, its rows of tiny peeling pink cottages. He feels a pang of regret. The more Luanne kicks, the smaller it gets. Soon, he thinks, it will look like a Monopoly piece. He feels himself panic and knows that's the worst thing he can do in a situation like this. His heart is beating so hard, he feels light-headed. Water forces its way down his throat. He coughs, frantic.

"Think good thoughts; don't panic," he tells himself and tries to reconstruct what Rainbow Village looked like so many years ago. When he was a kid. It was really pink back then, like flamingos, like sunsets.

What else is that pink?

Just then, a wave hits the raft. Salt sprays his face. He gags. Luanne continues her kicking. The raft is moving farther and farther away from shore. Waves break over it. Bill holds on to the edge of it. He can hardly breathe. His knuckles turn white. His hands feel weak.

That's when the smell of baby oil and Mercurochrome comes back to him.

And the pink of cherry lip gloss.

It was here, at Rainbow Village, that Bill had his first kiss. He'd told Luanne that part of the story, too.

The girl was eight years old. Wore her hair held back with pink plastic barrettes, same color as the tiny cabins. Her parents owned the place. He and the other boys called her Snow White because her hair and skin were that white. Her eyes were bleached blue.

"Albino," his mother said.

Bill thought that was a Spanish word for "beautiful."

He built her a sand castle decorated with scallop shells.

"Are you my Prince Charming?" she asked.

Bill told her everything. All of his secrets.

Some of his father's.

After Bill and his mother left Rainbow Village, he wrote her for more than a year. Told her the details of his life without her. His first bike. His first home run. When each letter was finished, he carefully addressed it. Gave it to his mother to mail.

The girl never wrote back, but Bill kept writing.

He couldn't help it. He'd grown accustomed to the quiet listening of it. No judgment passed. Just a weekly tally of joy and sorrow.

"Do you like football? I don't. Not really. Not after today." Every letter ended with the same question, "When can I see you again?"

The last letter Bill wrote was angry. He and his mother had been to the doctor. "Since you've gone I've grown smaller," he wrote. "Someday, I'll disappear."

When he handed the letter to his mother to mail, she wouldn't take it. "The girl is dead," she said. Bill never mentioned it again.

Luanne knows all about it—Snow White, the kiss, the castle. Everything.

So why are we here?

In the water, something slick brushes against Bill's leg. He looks down and sees a school of stingrays swimming just below the surface. There are a dozen or more, some the size of a small kite. Their tinfoil skin glints. "Don't move," Bill says. *One flick of their tail.*

The stingrays part around Bill and Luanne, gliding.

Luanne shakes her head. "They're more afraid of you than you of them."

She reaches down gently and picks a small one up by its fin. Places it between them on the raft. "Look," she says, "it's dying; you can tell by the skin."

The stingray is about the size of a man's wallet. Mottled gray. Still, Bill lets go of the raft. He doesn't want to be that close.

"That doesn't mean it can't still hurt you," he says. Dog-paddles furiously.

The ray's tail spins like radar. The raft bobs up and down in the waves, slams into Bill. "Maybe you should just put it back," he says, gulping water and air. Grabs the raft's edge before it knocks him out.

"It's dying from the inside out, you know?" she says and makes an odd cooing sound, like something fluttering in her throat. Luanne kisses the stingray; its tail just misses her cheek.

For a moment, Bill and Luanne hold onto the raft in silence. A storm in the distance gives the water energy. Waves chop like slaps. They can barely hang on.

"Did He hurt you again?" Bill says. "Is that what this is all about?"

She slips the stingray back into the water. It hesitates, then glides away.

She won't meet Bill's eye. Not good, he thinks. He wants to know what she's done but is afraid he already does. He looks back at the motor court, now a spot in the horizon. The water has turned cold.

Too deep, he thinks. *We're out too deep.* "Where will you go?" he says.

"Home."

"Take me with you."

She leans across and kisses his hand. He feels the dried salt of her lips.

"Are you sure?" she says. Bill nods. "Then don't let go of the rope."

And before he says another thing, she dives into the gray

green water. The rope yanks him down hard. Bill couldn't let go if he tried. His lungs are pins and needles. His heart beats in his head. The ocean is a tornado sky. His hands, wild, grasp at nothing. He knows Luanne is somewhere below him. The rope is still around his waist, pulling him deeper. Can't see her but feels her swimming hard. This is what it's like, he thinks. The Selkie.

Then all of a sudden, her lips are on his. She blows air into his lungs.

It's the last thing he remembers.

Hours later, when Bill finally comes to, it's dark. He's back in the room, tied to a Barcalounger with the bright yellow rope. The lifeline.

"Luanne?"

There's an egg-sized lump on his head. On his chest, a postcard. Vintage 1970s. The Rainbow Village he remembers. Luanne's loopy handwriting is on the back. He squints to read it.

"Love you."

He struggles with the ropes, but they cut tight into his arms. The postcard falls to the floor.

Outside, the traffic of Gulf Boulevard whispers by. The moon is pleated through the jalousie windows. It must be nearly morning, he thinks. This is the time of day Bill usually likes the most. The gray time: the time before dawn, when the gospel preachers sing sweet and low of redemption, of ecstasy. Curves come and go at ninety, ninety-five. Beauty queen smooth. Anything is possible.

"Luanne?"

He calls out louder, just in case she's somewhere in the small room, maybe sleeping on the cool of the yellowed linoleum floor or in one of the tiny twin beds.

She's gone.

Between the blinds, he can see the parking lot. The vapor lights of Gulf Boulevard cast it in fluorescent green. After a while, sunrise. Must be six o'clock, he thinks. *Somebody will be here soon.*

But no one comes. Bill realizes he can no longer feel the keys in the mesh pocket of his trunks. He looks out the window again. His truck is gone. He's actually not that surprised.

As the sun rises higher, heat builds in the small room, wears on him. He falls asleep and dreams he has fallen into a fire. His clothes and body burn, but it's not a nightmare. The flame is kind. Charred bits of him hang in the air, then catch the draft.

This must be love, he thinks.

When the cabin door finally opens, it's nearly noon. A small woman flips on a table lamp. The white shade is pasted with shells; a few fall away. She's carrying cleaning supplies.

"Oh," she says, "there was supposed to be some girl in here."

Bill blinks. "Can you give me a hand?"

The woman shakes her head, takes a step back out of the room. "I'm going to let the police sort this out," she says.

Bill's face goes hot. "It's just a joke. Please."

He knows the police are the last thing Luanne needs right now. "Haven't you ever played a crazy joke on someone?"

The woman surveys the scene cautiously. "Don't mess with crazy stuff," she says, then closes the door. Bill can hear her running across the broken-shell driveway.

"She's not crazy," he says, just to say it.

Bill looks around one last time. All her things are still there. The sandals. Her suitcase. He wants to take them. Pack them away in his attic. Knows he probably can't.

So he commits them, and this room, to memory. Misses it already.

◆

Waiting for the Hungarians

MY OLD NEIGHBORHOOD in Toledo was called Kuschwantz, although nobody's quite sure what that means anymore, or who first called it that. Everyone who lived there was from the Old Country. Polish. Catholic. English optional. We killed chickens in the backyard for dinner. My dad owned the garage. My uncle was the baker. My godfather was the milkman. Our dramas fit within the small of God's hand.

After I was born, my godfather made sure that the milk he delivered to our house had the thickest layer of cream floating on the top. We had more than anyone had, even the nuns.

When Mother Superior found out, she sent the parish priest to speak to my mother about the nature of my paternity. My mother wasn't from the neighborhood. After three brandies, he forgot why he came.

Our names were all unpronounceable to people who lived in other neighborhoods, but we knew the secrets of them. Not everyone's last name ended in "ski." Some were "witz." Some were "ka." We were ka: *Marchewka*, which means "carrot." Most of my family has orange red hair.

The Polish have quite a sense of humor.

We were leery of Hungarians, as a general rule. Their

food was too aromatic. They didn't really know how to polka. And they couldn't tell a joke right. They would say, "The Russians are insane but the Polish are crazy."

Everybody knows that the joke goes, "The Russians are insane but the Hungarians are crazy."

You have to feel sorry for a people who have no sense of humor.

For the most part, we distanced ourselves from them. This, of course, was before Jamie Farr mentioned Tony Packo's café on *M*A*S*H* and doomed us to an eternity of saying, "Yes. Packo's does have great Hungarian hot dogs," even though everyone knows that in the Old Country there is no such thing as a hot dog and the amount of garlic that Hungarians use is unseemly.

When I was nine years old, just a week into third grade, Hungarians suddenly became part of my life. One morning I came downstairs for breakfast, and my mother kissed my forehead, handed me a fresh jelly doughnut that she made herself, and said, "I've ironed all your clothes."

"Where's Dad?"

"Left early."

Then I walked to summer school, and my mother went to Florida. She left a note saying she was going to marry a Hungarian electrical engineer. I was surprised. I didn't even know they had electricity in Hungary.

It was 1967. The Summer of Love.

America is the land of cheerful inaccuracies.

That night my dad sat at the kitchen table and read the note over and over again.

"Shouldn't you make dinner?"

"Go to bed," he said.

So I called Nellie. She lived across the street. We were the same age. She always looked like a shadow: white skin, pale hair. She barely spoke. Her father worked nights at the Knights of Columbus as a bartender. On Saturdays, she would go with him to work and clean glasses off the tables. Drink whatever was left in them.

She wasn't my best friend, but she was the only other person I knew who didn't have a mother.

"I'll be right over," she said.

I climbed out my bedroom window and down the pear tree. We lay on our backs on the grass, and I told her all about the ironed clothes, the doughnuts, the note. She didn't say anything. We stared at the stars for a long time. The air was sticky sweet, filled with the smell of rotting pears. After a while I said, "Why did your mother leave?"

"Hungarians."

I think she just said that to make me feel better.

Did you know that Hungarians are the only people in Europe who use their family name first and birth name second? In Hungary, Steven Spielberg would introduce himself as Spielberg Steven. They are a very mysterious people.

After that first night, I was suddenly in charge of meals. I'd never cooked anything before, never even made a sandwich. Nellie said, "Don't panic. Just ask yourself: what would the Hungarians do?"

I understood.

Chicken paprikas, goulash, cabbage and noodles, slabs of

paprika bacon roasted over potatoes: with the aid of a public library cookbook, I fried, boiled, and rendered my way through the entire Finno-Ugric culinary palate.

I had no choice. My mother was more than 1,300 miles away cooking Hungarian food for someone else. My dad was hungry.

The food made him sweat.

At the end of September, he signed me up for Camp Fire Girls. It was the first troop we'd ever had in the neighborhood. "They meet after school. You won't have to cook," he said.

That night we were having tokany, a sour cream–based stew made of slab bacon, flank steak, pork, veal, and sausage, spiced with caraway and paprika. It was served over dumplings. If it hadn't been an unseasonably warm evening, low eighties, I think it would have been my best meal yet.

"But I like to cook," I said.

My dad pushed the fat flour dumpling around his plate. Didn't answer. He was still wearing his overalls from the garage, his name, *Roman*, embroidered in red letters over the pocket. The light over our kitchen table was too bright. Made him look pale, his blue eyes watery. He'd dyed his red hair black. It caught the light. Looked like oil.

"You don't like it?" I asked.

He shrugged. I looked away. Next door, in the Sobczaks' kitchen, they were having dinner, too. Our windows were directly across from each other, and you could see right in if no one pulled the curtains. No one ever pulled the curtains.

The Sobczaks had two girls, both in high school. Both pink and clean. Mrs. Sobczak was wearing a dress just like you see mothers on television wearing, like on that show *Father Knows Best*. It was white with a cherry print and a black patent belt around her tiny waist. She was serving a whole chicken, coleslaw, and tiny white rolls. It made my stomach growl.

Mr. Sobczak ran the funeral parlor. Like my dad, he'd just come home from work. He was still in his suit shirt, his sleeves rolled up, laughing. When the girls left the table, the parents leaned across the dinner plates and kissed. I'd never seen my own parents kiss like that. I turned away, embarrassed.

"Your mother wants you to come visit," my dad said. "Next summer. When she's settled. She's buying a house."

I wondered who would cook for him. "Will the Hungarian be there?"

"You'll leave in August," he said. Then pushed his plate away and left the room.

So I became a Camp Fire Girl.

Our troop was called *Ta-Wa-Deka*, which means "clever and smart and willing for anything." The third-grade class was small, so there were just four of us: Linda, Nellie, Vicki, and me. The only thing we were willing to do was watch television. Cheerful inaccuracies abounded.

Linda's parents were rich, and she lived in a big house near the park. Linda had real Hush Puppies and lace collars that her mother bought outside of the neighborhood, at Tiedtke's department store. She would have been very pretty, but she was always yelling at people: "Are you looking at me?"

They always were. It was hard not to. She had polio and wore braces on her legs, teeth, and one arm. She glinted.

The last of our troop was Vicki. Mrs. Williamson, her mom, was our troop leader. Vicki was my real best friend. She wore a thick layer of foundation, powder, and eye shadow at all times. Had an air of elementary school mystery and left a cloud of Evening in Paris wherever she went. She was the only girl with hair that was redder than mine.

Mrs. Williamson's hair was red, too. She always wore it in a twisted beehive with tiny pink bows stuck in here and there. "A contrasting accessory," she told us. Then explained that redheads should never wear pink, and that precisely is why she always did.

"More things are possible in the Land of No," she would tell us with great portent. Being third graders, we innately understood this philosophy.

Mrs. Williamson was an entire universe of cheerful inaccuracies. Never married, so not actually a "Mrs.," her last name was really Wojohowitz, but she sold Avon door to door in Ottawa Hills, the fancy section of Toledo, so Williamson it was.

Vicki, again because of Avon, had an old name, too. It was *Celestynka*, which means "from heaven." Mrs. Williamson was going for that whole virgin birth thing but eventually gave up when Vicki turned three and developed both an insatiable love of kielbasa and the butcher's hooked nose. This, of course, explained why a single mother could afford steak not just on Saturday nights but three times a week.

When nobody was around, I called her "Celestynka" or "Kielbasa Nose." She answered to both.

Avon was very good to Mrs. Williamson and Vicki. Not only did it provide them with cheerfully inaccurate names, but every week the company shipped a new box filled with samples. Vicki and I would spend Saturday afternoons trying everything on and pretending we were going to meet Davy Jones of the Monkees at Majewski's Five and Dime, where he would be buying all the *Teen Beat* magazines so he could send the pictures of himself to his mother.

"He'll want to marry us," Vicki would say. "And we can change our names to Jones; that's his real name."

The one time I pointed out that he wasn't an American and our parents would be angry, she said, "I'll convert him."

We were all slightly obsessed with the whole American thing.

Luther Gulick, MD, and his wife, Charlotte Gulick, founded the Camp Fire Girls in 1910 in Vermont. They chose the name *Camp Fire* because they believed that when people learned to make fire, they became a community.

Kuschwantz didn't need anybody from Vermont to help us build a community. We hardly left the neighborhood. We didn't need to. Our streets were filled with shops and bars and restaurants. Most of us were born in our own homes and buried in the church graveyard. Perfect symmetry.

But our parents wanted more for us. They wanted Camp Fire Girls: it was the most American thing they knew.

So while the other troops in other neighborhoods recited

the Camp Fire motto, "Wohelo: Work, Health, Love," we learned the elements of corporate strategy and investigated the economic impact of vertical integration and monopoly in American business.

As business guru Joseph Pratt said: "The 1960s is a good time to be in business in the United States, an era when American efficiency and entrepreneurship is the wonder of the world."

And we had the candy to prove it. Almond Roca Buttercrunch, Creamy Smooth Mint Patties, Almond Caramel Clusters, and the ever-popular P-Nuttles: it was our goal to move more boxes of this stuff than any other troop in America. We wore red, white, and blue uniforms and trained for it like Olympic athletes.

While we could have earned beads for completing activities in several areas like outdoors and science, we filled up on business beads until each and every tiny blue felt vest we wore was so heavily decorated that it looked like it could belong to General MacArthur. *The Camp Fire's Adventure Trails* guidebook set the bar high.

B-114: Ask a businessperson or lawyer to explain to you what a contract is. Find out how contracts are used.

B-197: Talk to a person who belongs to a union. Get this person's opinion on the usefulness of unions. Talk to someone else who does not belong to a union and get that person's opinion, too.

We were undaunted. We asked it all, took notes, and applied any glimmer of insight into creating a strategy for the sale of candies. We didn't have much time to prepare. The sale ran from the first week in February to the first week in March. The candies had to be ordered in January, unless you wanted to give them as Christmas gifts, which was encouraged, and so then your orders had to be placed in November. We had, essentially, two months to become captains of industry.

"Commitment is crucial," Mrs. Williamson told us. "You must commit your heart and soul to selling. You must feel the calling right down to your Keds."

The more boxes sold, the less you had to pay to go to camp. Most of us had never been downtown, let alone to "camp." A camp in Michigan near a cherry farm was heady stuff.

"You can swim in a lake and ride horses," Mrs. Williamson said. "They serve fresh-made pie and sing around a campfire and roast marshmallows."

"Do our fathers have to come?" Nellie asked.

"Just girls," Mrs. Williamson said.

"Girls are better," Nellie said in a very quiet voice.

Mrs. Williamson gave her a hug.

Apparently, our enthusiasm was unusual for a troop, even one whose name was Ta-Wa-Deka. Pretty soon, Mrs. Williamson received a memo from the home office.

"Diversify."

As an Avon representative, she understood that a good salesperson had to have a diverse background to think on her feet.

"Girls," she said, "we will modify our strategy." And soon we'd moved on to other badge categories, "modifying" as we went.

O-116: Recognize and identify several birds by their calls. Learn to imitate them.

This translated into "help Mrs. Williamson cold-call new clients." We would stake out streets in Ottawa Hills and make notes as to what time the husbands arrived home, what kind of car they drove, and if the women even wore makeup.

At the big houses, all of us went with her to the door. "These are my girls," she would say. "Being a widow, four is quite a challenge."

This was Nellie's cue. "Could we please have a glass of water?" she'd ask. "We haven't eaten all day."

Nellie was so thin and pale, the women believed her immediately. And if they didn't, she'd fall to the ground in a faux faint. And then we'd roll in Linda and her wheelchair to seal the deal.

"Are you looking at me?" she'd say and wave her arm brace at them.

The befuddled women would usually murmur apologies, serve up milk and cookies, and then load up on perfume glacé compacts and mallard duck decanters filled with aftershave for their husbands.

By Halloween, we were an über–sales force, committed down to our Keds. We had designed our business model and were ready. But Vicki and I were concerned. Mrs. Williamson had taught us that the first rule of business is to evaluate your market. Despite her enthusiasm—"Everybody in the neighborhood will want to help!"—we knew it wasn't going to be like raising money to buy pagan babies. There were no pictures of us with flies crawling up our noses. We didn't have to eat dirt. It was going to be a tough sell.

Worse than that, we had a candy store in the neighborhood. Nobody was going to want candies that came from any place other than Kuschwantz. It was clear to us that we had to expand our customer base.

"Hungarians," I said. "They will eat anything."

So the following Saturday, I met Vicki at the bus stop. We were going to find Hungarians.

She was late and out of breath. The bus pulled up, and we sat down in front. Vicki looked around to see if anyone was watching and then whispered, "My mom told me a secret and I *have* to tell you but you can't tell *anyone* and you can't act like you know. Okay? Cross your heart?"

I didn't like the sound of that. Vicki had a serious look on her face. But before she could say anything else, the bus stopped in front of the convent. Sister Jadwiga, the school librarian, got on.

On some level that wasn't surprising. Sister Jadwiga was not allowed to drive anymore. Over the Thanksgiving holiday, when she was visiting the motherhouse in Kraków, she was arrested for driving a tractor into the bedroom of a nearby home owned by her childhood sweetheart and his new wife. Poland banned her for life, even though her visit was actually historic. Sister Jadwiga was one of the first people ever to participate in a Breathalyzer test. And even though she failed, there was still something thrilling about it for the rest of us.

She sat down between us. When she did, her coat came open, and I could see that she wasn't wearing her habit, just a dress, but she had on her veil. "Where are you girls going?" she asked us. Seemed distracted.

"To find Hungarians," Vicki said.

"Where are you going, Sister?" I asked her.

"To find Jesus."

That's when we noticed that Sister Jadwiga was carrying a small square suitcase.

"Do you think he's with the Hungarians?" Vicki asked.

Sister Jadwiga seemed to think about that for a minute, then turned to me and said, "You're the one whose mother left. Is that right?"

Vicki looked away, quickly, out the bus window. I nodded.

"I suppose you are you going to Florida to live with her now?" she asked.

I had the sudden urge to say yes, but it wasn't true. It was just a vacation—and I even hated to think about it. All I could imagine was my father sitting at the dinner table alone.

Sister Jadwiga must have seen that in my face. She looked out the window, at the dirty snow on the drab streets. Not at us. Then said, "Love makes people do strange things."

The bus stopped at the corner. The doors opened. Vicki grabbed my hand. "This is our stop, Sister," she said. "Tell Jesus we send our love."

"Close call," Vicki said as the cloud of black exhaust covered us. "You know how nuns are. She'd find the first drugstore and call our parents, and then we'd never be able to do the market evaluation and nobody—not Linda or you or me or anybody—will ever get to camp."

I didn't understand why we left Sister Jadwiga. She seemed so lonely. As the bus pulled away, she took off her veil. Shook her head. I was surprised that her hair was red, too. Just like mine.

"There's always next year," I said to Vicki. "If we don't make our goals, we can readjust them. We can make them next year."

She shook her head. "I don't think there's going to be a next year. One of Mom's new ladies is a social worker for Lucas County. She asked about one of us. Mom won't tell me who, but it can't be Linda because her parents are rich and rich people never do stuff like that. So it has to be Nellie."

I thought about this for a minute. Nellie's dad had a new girlfriend that he met at the Knights of Columbus. When she came over, Nellie would dress up in the clothes her mother left behind and stand on the front porch. Wouldn't come in. It was cold, too.

I could see her standing there in that faded flowered housedress, the red roses worn nearly white. It was four sizes too big and caught the wind like a sail. I could hear her father yelling at her, "Come inside! People will think you're crazy!"

"I'm waiting," she'd yell back.

I knew what she was waiting for. I was waiting, too.

"You know," Vicki said. "When they ask about you, you're as good as gone."

"It doesn't mean anything," I said, but I was lying.

"It means The Home."

She was right. The Children's Home was an orphanage. If you couldn't take care of your children, and there was no one to help you, you signed them over to the home.

"So what do we do?" I asked.

"Sell," Vicki said.

There was only one problem. Our Hungarian market was somewhere on the other side of town, and the bus was gone, and we were not in Kuschwantz anymore. It took us both a minute to get our bearings.

"*Dorr* Street," Vicki said quietly.

I looked at the street sign, and it was. The nuns warned us never to go to Dorr Street because it was dangerous, but I'd been there a lot. It never looked dangerous to me: there was a grocery store, clothing shop, and movie theater; people were everywhere. It was a tiny city within a city. It looked a lot like Kuschwantz, except for the fact that there wasn't a single white person, except for us.

"What do we do?"

"We'll wait for the next bus," I said.

"But—"

"They're just like us," I said, because that's what my dad had told me. Since his garage was at the edge of Kuschwantz, on the corner of Junction and Dorr streets, he worked on cars from both neighborhoods. He liked to barter. He fixed the First Pentecostal Church of Christ's bus in exchange for catfish suppers for his mechanics. Once the word got out, all the churches would bring their buses and vans to him. And some members of the congregations brought their cars, too.

On Saturdays, before my mother left, my dad and I would drive through the neighborhood and pick up sweet potato pies, fried chicken, and, of course, catfish dinners. The churches always served lunch after choir rehearsal on Saturday, and they always needed a bus, or van, or car fixed. Sometimes we'd stop at a house and my dad would run in and come back with two dozen eggs or a quart of honey. People would shout at us on the street, "Hey, Romy! Who's your girlfriend?" and my dad would pull over and talk.

I suddenly realized that we hadn't driven down Dorr Street in a long time. I didn't know why. And Dad never brought home food anymore. Never talked about his friends here.

It began to snow hard. Fat, wet flakes soaked our wool scarves and gloves. Vicki's mascara was running down her face. She was shivering. People began to stare. Some whispered.

"I don't like this," she told me.

"Let's walk."

Vicki looked like she was going to cry. "Nothing will happen," I said but didn't feel as sure. The dark, low clouds made the morning seem threatening. The wind was picking up. "My dad's garage isn't far from here." I wasn't sure that was true. I hadn't watched for the cross streets. But I was pretty sure that if we started walking, we'd find our way.

"Walk like you think you know where you're going," Vicki said. "That's what my mom always told me."

So we did. We walked fast and determined. The wind kicked up, and soon it was clear that the heavy flakes had turned into a snowstorm. The streetlights above us flicked on. The streets quickly became deserted. I grabbed Vicki's hand, and we ran blind. My lungs ached. We ran block after block, and then I suddenly realized that we'd been running the wrong way. My dad's garage was in the opposite direction.

Vicki started sobbing. "We'll just backtrack," I said. But I was so cold that I couldn't imagine walking any farther. Suddenly, I heard the sound of laughing, singing. "It's a church," I said, grabbing her hand and running toward the sound.

As we got closer, we could see people entering a storefront. Warm light from the open door shone on their faces. There was a tall, thin woman in a long, black choir robe greeting the congregation.

"Children, what are you doing so far from home?" she said when she saw us.

"Looking for Hungarians," Vicki said.

Mrs. Williamson would have been proud. Lost in a blizzard, Vicki was still focused and committed to the sale of candy.

The woman threw her head back and laughed. "Honey, I have no idea where they would be. I can't tell you people apart. Where on Earth are your mamas?"

"Do you know Romy?" I asked.

"The car man? Everybody knows Romy the car man."

And so she called my dad. While we waited for him to

come, she sat with us on the bench near the door. "You're father's a good man," she told me. "But he has *got* to stop calling us 'colored people.' He could get shot for that kind of thing."

When Dad finally came, he was furious at us.

"Romy, you best keep an eye on these girls," the woman told him.

He flushed. It seemed like he wanted to say something, but didn't. He thanked her for taking care of us and apologized. Once we got in the truck, he slapped me so hard across the face that his hand was imprinted on my check for three days.

After that, I never spent a minute alone.

Since my grandparents were dead and my uncle was a bachelor, the ladies of the neighborhood took turns caring for me after school and on Saturdays. Mrs. Kaminski, who always smelled like bread dough and jam, watched me until I accidentally started a kitchen towel on fire. Then the curtains. And then the rug, which even she admitted didn't belong so close to the stove. The next month, I stayed with Mrs. Wozohowik. Everyone agreed it wasn't my fault that her boy was nearly electrocuted. My dad taught me how to rewire a toaster. His didn't. It was that simple. Besides, it's not like he died. It just knocked him out. No harm done.

The candy sale went as expected. No one bought. No one could figure out why we wanted to go to camp when there was a park in the neighborhood. We sold ten boxes total, mostly to our parents, and then disbanded.

We never talked to each other much after that.

After the Dorr Street incident, Vicki's mother forbade her to go anywhere with me. Or even to speak to me. I later heard that Linda was sent to the Children's Home.

Every now and then, I'd see Nellie in her mother's dress standing on her front porch across the street. One time, my dad closed the living room drapes.

"Kid's a drunk," he said. "It's that mother's fault."

Even though I was grounded for the rest of the school year, my dad cut my hair short, bought me blue jeans, and took me to work with him on Saturdays. "You need to learn to take this place over someday," he told me. "You're the only son I have."

He laughed when he said it, but we both knew it was true. And so, I pumped gas. He taught me how to change a tire and charge a battery. After work, Dad and I would sit at the kitchen table and eat TV dinners and talk about football and cars. We'd settle into an easy silence.

The last day of school, I came home and saw that my father had packed all my clothes into every suitcase we had and left them by the door.

I called Nellie.

"You're never coming back," she said.

"It's just a vacation."

"That's what my mother said."

"My dad wouldn't lie," I said, but I wasn't sure. Even my winter coats were packed.

"Hungarians are everywhere," she said and hung up the phone.

When Dad came home from work that night, he had

a sack of Tony Packo's Hungarian hot dogs with him. We'd never had them before. They weren't like the chili dogs we usually got. They weren't real hot dogs at all. They were hot sausages smothered in some sort of spicy sauce, mustard, and onions and served with a sweet hot pepper relish. He also bought a side order of paprikas dumplings with gravy and sauerkraut.

"They're not so bad," he said.

"I thought you said August."

"The courts said different. Girls need a mother."

It took me a moment to understand what he was saying. Nellie was right. I wasn't coming back. Ever. And he knew, the entire time. He knew.

"I didn't want to make it harder. To upset you."

His voice cracked when he said this. I couldn't even look at him. *He knew.*

Across the street at Nellie's house, the porch light went on. "What, is she drunk again?" my dad said. We went to the window. Nellie was wearing her mother's faded dress.

"That kid just isn't right anymore."

That's when I noticed it. "The house is on fire."

It was true. Fire was suddenly winding itself around the front curtains. The porch light popped.

My dad and I both stood there for a moment, watching as if dreaming.

"Damn mother," he finally said, and ran to the basement to get the fire extinguisher. "Call the fire department," he shouted at me.

I wanted to call, but I couldn't stop watching.

The fire spilled onto the porch, but she just stood there. Maybe in shock. Maybe drunk. Maybe just waiting.

All of Kuschwantz was running toward Nellie. The small house lit up the night.

I stepped outside. She slowly waved when she saw me. I waved back one last time, and the thick smoke billowed out into the street, blanketed the stars. It tinted the night sepia, as if the moment had already been lived and forgotten.

◆

···

The Last Rites

···

ZIMMER HAD ALWAYS WANTED to be buried in his 1953
Cadillac Eldorado convertible. Built the year he was born,
only 532 of these cars were ever made. The name *Eldorado*
came to Cadillac's marketing division by way of the Spanish
el dorado, meaning "gilded one" or "golden man," depending
on the buyer. The instrument inserts, door moldings, and
kick strips were all fourteen-carat-gold plated.

Zimmer had twelve gold records, a Golden Globe, and
a gold Oscar statuette.

12 + 1 + 1 = 14

It made perfect sense.

The Eldorado came in only a handful of colors; Zimmer's
was Aztec red with East Indian red pepper leather seats.
When he drove down the streets of Los Angeles, the Caddie's
enormous fins made it look like a school of embarrassed
sharks circling aimlessly in barren waters.

He didn't often drive it. On tour, he usually trailered it
behind his bus, just for photo opportunities. It was handy
when he needed it. And he always needed it. Toward the
end, Zimmer spent most of his days sitting in the driver's
seat, not driving, just listening to the radio or sometimes the
static of a station, the ghost announcer fading in and out.

Since Zimmer died while still a legal resident of LA, a car-crazed city that has drive-in churches, drive-in bars, an ill-fated drive-in tattoo parlor, and some of the last remaining drive-in movie theaters in America, it was a given that his last wish would be granted. The fact that the Turtle Island Casino Theme Park in Orlando, Florida, was his benefactor was unforeseen, but understandable.

There was no next of kin. He died while still under contract to the casino. In fact, while still in their parking garage. The casino felt he owed them. And he did. His bar bill alone was enormous.

The funeral arrangements were quickly made. His name was still on the marquee, so all they had to do was add "The Last Show" underneath. There was a twenty-dollar cover charge and two-drink minimum. No exceptions. They wouldn't even comp Janet in.

"I'm all he had," she told the box office manager, a young woman wearing a Pocahontas costume that amounted to a couple of strategically placed scraps of suede and a few chaste feathers. "I'm the only one who really loved him," Janet said.

The box office manager adjusted her suede, giggled, and then laughed out loud.

Apparently, Zimmer had not been lonely while in Orlando.

"Never mind," Janet said, and knew she should have taken the time to dye her gray hair, buy a new black dress, and lose about 27.5 pounds. But there hadn't been time. It all happened so fast. No one expected Zimmer to die—not ever.

Zimmer was an American original—the tight pants, the cowboy swagger, the ill-tempered snarl. When he sang, he channeled Elvis, crawled inside that rockabilly sound and turned it inside out, made it his own. By the time Zimmer had his first gold record, he'd moved to LA, lost touch with Janet, bought a mansion in the Hollywood Hills, and opened a line of credit at the local Tiffany & Co., which he used with such lavish abandon that they ran out of little blue boxes at Christmas.

What Zimmer didn't know is that the average shelf life of musicians is about ten years—after that they still perform and record, but nobody cares. At thirty, his label dropped him and he took up acting—mostly horror films and straight-to-video westerns.

When Zimmer turned forty-one, he was cast as a washed-up rock star in an independent film, found what critics called his "white hot center," and won both the Golden Globe and Oscar. He'd also found Janet again. Called her from the *Vanity Fair* party.

"My own sorrow saved me," he said.

Ten years later, he was playing supermarket openings and casinos again. But a core of his fans remained, a couple hundred or so, many of them willing to pay twenty dollars a head to get close to a man whose blood was now replaced with embalming fluid. The line wrapped around the casino; some had camped out all night.

Still, that really wasn't what made Janet uneasy. It was something about seeing Zimmer dressed in his trademark dark sunglasses, the long straggly hair curling beneath his white Stetson hat, and that exquisite Nudie jacket, hand-tailored by Nudie Cohen himself, the one with the rhinestone-encrusted image of Christ crucified at Calvary across the back and the archangels standing watch on both arms, that unnerved her.

She wasn't exactly sure what bothered her about it; the jacket was somewhat in keeping with the gravity of the moment. *At least he wasn't wearing that Vargas Girl silk shirt,* she thought, and then immediately suspected that probably he was wearing it underneath his jacket.

That was the kind of man Zimmer was: Jesus up front, naked pinups close to his heart.

Maybe the problem was that Janet expected him to be lying in the backseat. Or, perhaps, laid out in the massive trunk.

But he wasn't.

Zimmer was propped up in the driver's seat with his hands discreetly wired onto the hand-sewn, East Indian red pepper leather steering wheel. Lips sewn into a crooked smile.

It was a Porter Wagoner dreamscape from which there was no waking. It was enough to make Janet drop her hot dish.

"Where should I put this?" she asked a man whose nametag read "Brother Billy." Janet assumed he was the preacher; he had an Ichabod Crane air about him. He tugged at the bottom of his coat jacket, cocked an eyebrow, leaned into the dish, sniffed, and said, "And what is *this* exactly?"

"Cold," Janet said.

And it was. Even though the flight from Minneapolis took three hours and fourteen minutes, and the Orlando traffic was so bad around the Disney exits that it was an hour taxi ride from the airport, her chicken and mushroom soup wild rice hot dish, the one she made only for special occasions, was still frozen in the center.

"And I'm going to need a microwave," she said.

Brother Billy looked confused.

"It was his favorite," she explained.

He turned away, unhelpful, and joined a group in the crowd who were mostly tattooed, mostly young, and mostly too thin. *Probably his LA friends,* she thought. They reminded Janet of the state fair sideshow, back when there was such a thing. She loved the sideshow. "Did you know that Teddy Roosevelt gave his 'speak softly and carry a big stick' speech in 1901 at the Minnesota State Fair?" she asked a tall woman, maybe a Nigerian, who had an ocelot wrapped around her neck like a shawl.

"I did not," the woman said coolly and stared at the sweating Pyrex in Janet's hands.

"Did you know that Bob Dylan was from Minnesota?" Janet said.

"Are you with *someone?*" the woman asked, and the way she asked, the way she said the word *someone,* expanding it, made it clearly mean "someone famous"—not just *any* someone.

"Zimmer," Janet said. The ocelot yawned. The woman slipped back into the crowd.

Zimmer and Janet were the same age exactly. They were

both born in the same hospital on the same day in the min-ing town of Hibbing on Minnesota's iron range. Zimmer was not his real name. He took it from Bob Dylan, who was born Robert Zimmerman and lived in a nondescript wooden house at the end of Zimmer's block.

By the time they reached junior high, Dylan had burned out the first time, but once a year on his birthday his fans, in-cluding Janet and Zimmer, made pilgrimages to his old house, lit candles, sang "Blowin' in the Wind," and cried be-cause they knew an era had passed.

Janet always baked a hot dish.

And now, hot dish in hand, she wanted to cry but wasn't sure it was appropriate. The sound system was playing Zim-mer's rendition of "Great Balls of Fire" over and over again— on a continuous loop.

Goodness gracious, was all she could think.

The Turtle Island Casino Theme Park was not a casino in the Vegas sense of the word. There were no poker tables. No dice. No baccarat. Decorated in a faux Native American motif, it was more like a bingo hall with slot machines. It had a twenty-four-hour, all-you-can-eat taco buffet and a five-hundred-seat performance hall that, six days a week, featured many once famous acts, like Zimmer, and on Thursdays hosted a martial arts amateur night cage fight that always was a sellout.

For Zimmer's "last show," all the seats had been removed. There were several bars lining the performance hall, all do-ing brisk business. Zimmer and his Eldorado were placed on a revolving platform in the center of the room. A large spotlight hung down from the rafters, making Zimmer and his car seem somewhat celestial, as if Jesus's own battered heart had finally softened to him.

Goodness gracious.

Janet suddenly had the urge to run, run all the way home, back to Hibbing, back behind her parent's garage where they shared their first kiss, when a woman stepped out of the crowd, lifted the lid off the Pyrex, and said, "Is there wild rice in this?"

Janet had never seen the woman before. In fact, she'd never even seen anything *like* her before. She was squat and fit, like a wrestler. Shocking blue eyes with a salt-and-pepper crew cut. She was wearing a Zimmer tank top from his Always Alone tour that made her breasts seem mammoth and somewhat mesmerizing. Or maybe it wasn't the shirt so much as the tattoo of Zimmer himself across her chest, staring down and grinning, his name and hers, "Reba" entwined in a heart.

"Reba?" Janet said.

Reba touched the heart and smiled. "This tat was his favorite of them all."

Janet couldn't help noticing that there were quite a lot to choose from. Reba had tattoos of Zimmer at various ages everywhere on her body—not just her cleavage but also her neck, both arms, *and God knows where else,* Janet thought. The scent of patchouli was overwhelming.

Reba leaned in and sniffed the hot dish. "He's allergic to wild rice," she said.

"Was," Janet corrected. "He *was* allergic . . ." It was a word that she had to begin to get used to. "But it wasn't rice; it was wheat." Janet took the lid back and placed it on the dish.

"That's right," Reba said. "I get them confused. Well. His real name really was Harold; did you know that?"

Janet, of course, did. And all the "z-wives," as he had called his fans, also knew that. So she lied. "No, I didn't."

Reba was triumphant.

Janet had seen it all before and knew it was time to walk away. Ever since the early eighties, z-wives followed Zimmer around the country. Most were just hoping to have their pictures taken with him—a meet and greet, as it's called. Some hoped for so much more. Some even stalked him.

"I didn't really know Zimmer that well," Janet said, and knew that was probably true.

She started to walk away, but Reba grabbed her arm. "Well," she said, "we were very close. If you know what I mean." And then she laughed a knowing laugh.

And Janet snapped.

"You delusional bitch," she began, and rambled on with the story of their simultaneous births; the Bob Dylan hot dish ritual; the fact that Zimmer could recite from the King James Bible and secretly believed every word of it; how Zimmer had encouraged her to change her own name, too.

"Call yourself *Daisy*," he told me. "If you call yourself *Daisy*, then you can travel around the country selling daisies at all my gigs. Everybody needs a hook."

She explained that she forgave him this transgression because it was the 1970s, "and that explained a lot." And so she remained *Janet*, because Janet was her mother's favorite name, and then became a labor relations lawyer. And never left home.

At this point, a busload of women, z-wives, had encircled them. They were wearing an array of concert t-shirts; many had tattoos. One was a nun, in full regalia.

They were all his women, Janet thought, then said, "And we loved each other, but we could never be together because he'd become lost . . . he'd become Zimmer. And as soon as he'd become Zimmer, he didn't belong to me anymore—he belonged to you."

The truth of the statement surprised Janet.

Reba looked stunned. "I'm sorry," she said gently. Then gave Janet a bear hug that lifted the hot-dish-carrying labor relations lawyer up off her feet and into the tattoo of Zimmer grinning across Reba's chest. It also toppled the hot dish.

The Pyrex lid splintered, sending shards of glass everywhere. Congealed wild rice and chicken fell in a mound at their feet.

I'm one of them, Janet thought. *A z-wife.*

For a moment, they all looked at her. They seemed to want her to say something, anything, as long as it was about Zimmer—just one more thing they could carry with them.

Overhead he sang, "You rattle my brain." Then a voice interrupted, called for a clean-up crew.

And they were still waiting, so Janet continued. "He called me the night he died," she said. "He said an astrologist was giving him a reading that day and suddenly stopped.

"She said she saw a wall of rain, and behind it was John

Lennon, and he spoke to him. 'Zimmer,' he said, 'It's not so bad on this side.'

"I told him to write a song about it. He laughed and said, 'I'm not Bono.'"

And the women laughed, too.

Janet walked away, out of the room, into the casino to get some air. On the wall next to the slot machines there was a sign: "The History of Turtle Island."

> Turtle Island is a sacred place, named after Grandmother Turtle, the Ancient One. According to legend, Maheo, the Creator, asked Grandmother Turtle to help him build a world, something to rule over. The Ancient One agreed. So Maheo mounded dirt and clay and stones and twigs around Grandmother Turtle until she became the hill, the mountain, the island, the Earth. It was an act of love, an act of sacrifice. At Turtle Island, we honor the act of sacrifice.

Lemon. Bar. Cherry, Janet thought. *No luck. No luck.*

In the corner of the massive room, a woman on a respirator was pulling slots at a dollar a shot. Her wheelchair hugged the machine, metal on metal. Her eyes were red with attention. Her breathing tube lay in her lap like a snake sunning itself.

Ding. Ding. Ding. No luck.

Janet looked into her coin cup. Quarters were as scarce as words.

The old woman took one last pull: three cherries appeared. A siren blared. Quarters streamed from the machine; they rolled and rolled until time seemed to stop. In their frenzied jingle dance, they rolled over the old woman;

her breathing tube parted their flow. Quarters and quarters, a silver river with two streams falling onto her lap, then onto the floor, piling quickly at her feet. The old woman seemed rooted in them.

She was quickly becoming a mountain, an Earth, an old Grandmother Turtle.

By now, everyone in the casino was watching the stream of silver, seemingly endless. Their dreams were sucked into its current, its undertow: some were cheering, some sweating, some wanted to help, some just wanted.

At the core of this, the old woman seemed unaware. She picked up four quarters, dropped them into the slot, and pulled the lever again, hard.

Lemon. Lemon. Bell, Janet thought. *No luck. No luck.*

After that, things became a blur.

Later, Janet would not remember running through the casino and back into the auditorium. She would not recall jumping onto the revolving platform and into the 1953 Cadillac Eldorado convertible—nor fastening her seatbelt nor starting the engine nor laying on the horn. Nor would she remember leaning into Zimmer, taking control of the wheel, and telling everybody to get out of the way.

But the bright light shone down on her, and the crowd parted.

And security opened the loading dock doors. And Janet punched the accelerator, and the box office manager, in her Pocahontas suedes, waved at Zimmer as she drove past.

They let her drive away—there wasn't much gas, after all. And they had called the police.

The only thing Janet would remember was the feeling of her hand on his, just like in the old days, and driving fast and reckless to nowhere in particular, and yet into each other's hearts.

Outside, high above the casino's parking lot, the skywriter took his last turn, added an exclamation point to the words "Jesus Loves You." Then flew away.

Janet watched him in the rearview mirror until the letters dissipated, expanded into the clouds—until the words faded away. Then drove as far as she could.

◆

ACKNOWLEDGMENTS

Over the past decade, some of these stories have appeared in other forms. I'd like to thank the editors of *Zoetrope ASE, Atlantic Monthly Unbound, One Story, Verb, West Branch, Chattahoochee Review,* and the *Mississippi Review* for picking me out of their respective slush piles. Many thanks also to Katherine Minton and Joanne Woodward at National Public Radio's "Selected Shorts" and Allan Gurganus and Kathy Pories at *New Stories of the South: The Year's Best, 2006* for giving "Jubilation, Florida" a life of its own. I'd also like to thank my editor Pamela McClanahan for loving all these stories and bringing them to print with such great care. Special thanks also goes to fellow writer Susan O'Neill, who took the time to read many of these and toss out the parts that needed to be tossed. And a final thanks to my springer spaniels Tyler and Fitzgerald—they don't read, they don't edit, and they have never done a voice-over in their lives, but I still love them madly.

A Travel Guide for Reckless Hearts
was designed and set in type at
Borealis Books by Will Powers.
The text typeface is Whitman,
designed by Kent Lew.
Printed by Sheridan Books.